Carmilla

The Original Vampire Romance –
A Haunting Gothic Tale of Love and Horror

A Modern Translation

Adapted for the Contemporary Reader

J. Sheridan Le Fanu

Translated by Tim Zengerink

Table of Contents

Preface - Message to the Reader

What If You Could Help Rebuild the Greatest Library in Human History?

Thousands of years ago, the Library of Alexandria stood as the crown jewel of human achievement — a sanctuary where the collected wisdom of every known civilization was gathered, preserved, and shared freely.

And then, it was lost.

Through fire, conquest, and the slow erosion of time, humanity lost not just books — but ideas, dreams, discoveries, and stories that could have changed the world forever.

Today, the Library of Alexandria lives again — and you are invited to be a part of its restoration.

Our mission is simple yet profound:

To rebuild the greatest library the world has ever known, and to translate all timeless works into every language and dialect, so that no seeker of knowledge is ever left behind again.

By joining our movement to rebuild the modern Library of Alexandria, you become part of an unprecedented mission:

- **Unlimited Access to the Greatest Audiobooks & eBooks Ever Written:**

  Instantly explore thousands of legendary works—Plato, Shakespeare, Jane Austen, Leo Tolstoy, and countless more. All instantly available to read or listen, placing a complete literary universe at your fingertips.

- **Beautiful Paperback & Deluxe Editions at Printing Cost**

  Own any title as an elegant paperback, deluxe hardcover, or stunning collectible boxset—offered to you at true printing cost, delivered straight to your door. Build your personal Library of Alexandria, crafted for beauty, built for durability, and worthy of proud display.

- **Fresh Translations for Modern Readers—in Every Language & Dialect**

  Enjoy timeless masterpieces reimagined in clear, contemporary language—no more outdated phrases or obscure references. Alongside the original versions, we're tirelessly translating these classics into every language and dialect imaginable, ensuring accessibility and understanding across cultures and generations.

- **Join a Global Renaissance of Literature & Knowledge**

  You directly support expanding our library, publishing deluxe editions at true cost, translating works into all global languages, and bringing humanity's greatest stories to people everywhere. By joining today, you're not just preserving a legacy of masterpieces; you set in motion a powerful wave of literary accessibility.

Become a Torchbearer of Knowledge.

Join us for free now at **LibraryofAlexandria.com**

Together, we will ensure that the light of human wisdom never fades again.

With gratitude and a shared love of knowledge,

The Modern Library of Alexandria Team

Visit:

www.libraryofalexandria.com

Or scan the code below:

Introduction

The Birth of the Female Vampire:
Seduction, Subversion, and the Supernatural

Before Bram Stoker's Dracula captured the literary world's imagination with its suave and sinister vampire, there was Carmilla—J. Sheridan Le Fanu's haunting and provocative novella that redefined Gothic horror and introduced one of literature's earliest and most compelling vampire figures. First published in 1872 as part of the collection In a Glass Darkly, Carmilla predated Dracula by twenty-five years and shaped the archetype of the vampire in key ways that Stoker would later adapt and popularize. Yet despite its influence, Carmilla stands apart as a work of deeply sensual dread, psychological nuance, and unsettling intimacy.

At its core, Carmilla is a tale of mystery and growing horror set in a secluded castle in Styria, Austria. It is narrated by Laura, a young woman who lives a quiet, isolated life with her father until the enigmatic Carmilla enters their lives under the guise of convalescence. Carmilla's arrival is the catalyst for a slow but inexorable descent into fear and fascination. As Laura is drawn ever closer to the strange and beautiful visitor, mysterious deaths spread throughout the region, and long-buried secrets begin to surface.

What makes Carmilla so groundbreaking is not merely its vampiric theme, but the nature of the relationship at its center. The bond between Laura and Carmilla is tinged with forbidden desire, emotional intensity, and ambiguous attraction. At a time when Victorian norms demanded strict sexual and gender conformity, Carmilla dared to explore female intimacy, longing, and identity through the metaphor of vampirism. Le Fanu's vampire is not the grotesque monster of folklore, but a refined, elegant, and seductive figure—a being who uses affection and charm to penetrate the social defenses of her victims.

This deeply psychological portrayal of horror marked a shift in Gothic literature. Rather than relying on external threats—such as ghosts, haunted mansions, or demonic possessions—Carmilla turns inward, suggesting that the greatest terrors lie within the self: within repressed desire, fear of the unknown, and the collapse of boundaries between self and other. The horror in Carmilla is as much emotional and existential as it is supernatural.

Le Fanu's genius lies in his ability to sustain suspense and unease through suggestion and atmosphere. The narrative unfolds slowly, with dread creeping in through hints and allusions rather than overt acts of violence. The castle, the surrounding forest, the strange dreams, and the uncanny resemblance between Carmilla and a long-dead ancestor all contribute to a sense of disorientation and decay. The reader, like Laura, is never quite sure what is real and what is imagined—until it is too late.

In many ways, Carmilla is both a product of its time and a subversion of it. While it reflects Victorian concerns about disease, sexuality, and the erosion of social order, it also defies conventional morality by presenting a vampire who is both villain and victim, predator and object of sympathy. Carmilla's fate, though necessary within the logic of the plot, is also tragic. She is punished not only for being a vampire but for embodying a kind of femininity and autonomy that Victorian culture sought to suppress.

Translated by Tim Zengerink

A Reflection of Victorian Anxieties
and Gothic Traditions

To understand the cultural power of Carmilla, it is essential to situate it within the Victorian worldview. The 19th century was a time of dramatic change: scientific advances, the decline of religious authority, the rise of the middle class, and the tightening grip of rigid moral codes all created a landscape of anxiety and contradiction. In particular, the figure of the vampire began to evolve in the literary imagination. No longer just a creature of Eastern European folklore, the vampire became a symbol of more abstract fears—of contagion, corruption, and moral ambiguity.

Le Fanu's Carmilla channels these concerns with remarkable subtlety. At the time of its publication, tuberculosis—then known as consumption—was ravaging Europe. The symptoms of vampirism in the novella, including languor, pallor, and wasting away, closely resemble those of the disease. In this way, the vampire becomes a metaphor for both literal and moral contagion, infecting not only the body but the soul. Carmilla's touch, her closeness, even her gaze, all seem to drain life from Laura—yet Laura cannot help but yearn for it.

The novella also engages with gender roles and the repression of female sexuality. Laura and Carmilla's relationship is laced with romantic and erotic undertones, making the story one of the earliest depictions of lesbian attraction in Western literature. Although the narrative never names their relationship explicitly, the emotional intensity and physical intimacy between the two women defy the era's norms of acceptable female behavior. Carmilla's seduction is not merely physical; it is emotional, intellectual, and spiritual. She disrupts Laura's sense of self, challenging her understanding of love, identity, and morality.

This subversion is what gives Carmilla its enduring resonance. The vampire is not just a monster but a force that reveals the fragility of societal boundaries. Carmilla blurs the line between the living and the dead, the innocent and the guilty, the natural and the unnatural. She forces her victims—and the readers—to confront uncomfortable truths about desire, otherness, and control.

Le Fanu's prose style enhances this effect. Unlike the sensationalism found in some Gothic fiction of the time, Carmilla is restrained, atmospheric, and poetic. The horror emerges not from shock but from mood—from the slow unraveling of certainty, the erosion of trust, and the encroaching sense of doom. Le Fanu masterfully constructs a world in which the supernatural and the psychological become indistinguishable, inviting readers to question the boundaries of reality itself.

The novella's epistolary structure—framed as a retrospective confession—adds to the complexity. Laura's narrative is colored by memory, trauma, and repression. Her voice is measured, almost clinical at times, but beneath the surface lies a deep well of grief and unresolved longing. She is both a survivor and a mourner, trying to make sense of something that defies logic and morality. In this way, Carmilla is also a story about the aftershocks of trauma—about how the past continues to haunt, possess, and shape the present.

Carmilla's Legacy and Continued Influence

Carmilla has left an indelible mark on vampire literature, film, and culture. Bram Stoker was undoubtedly influenced by Le Fanu's tale when crafting Dracula. The themes of seduction, disease, and foreign intrusion reappear in Stoker's novel, as do narrative devices such as the isolated setting, the helpless victim, and the vampire's dual nature. But where Dracula embraces a male-dominated world of action, resistance, and conquest, Carmilla dwells in the realm of the interior—of emotions, secrets, and unspoken fears.

In the years since its publication, Carmilla has been reinterpreted and adapted countless times, particularly within feminist and queer literary circles. Scholars and artists have recognized in Carmilla a figure of both oppression and empowerment—one who defies patriarchal norms, asserts her own desires, and exists outside the boundaries of traditional womanhood. While early readers may have seen her as a threat to moral order, modern audiences often view her as a tragic antihero—a woman punished for daring to be different.

This modern translation preserves the haunting beauty of Le Fanu's original prose while updating the language to be accessible for contemporary readers. It aims to capture the emotional complexity, moral ambiguity, and lyrical quality that define the novella. Archaic expressions have been clarified, sentence structures have been streamlined, and obscure references have been gently modernized—without altering the tone, setting, or narrative integrity.

Reading Carmilla today is not simply an exercise in literary history; it is a confrontation with the timeless themes of love, loss, identity, and power. The story asks difficult questions: What does it mean to desire someone who may destroy you? What does it mean to be different in a world that demands conformity? What is the price of closeness, and how do we protect ourselves from the dangers that lie not in monsters, but in intimacy itself?

This edition invites you to step into the shadowy world of Styria, where twilight lingers, secrets fester, and the boundaries between affection and annihilation blur. It is a world where horror wears the face of beauty, where comfort hides danger, and where the dead do not rest quietly. In Carmilla, the vampire is not a distant threat—it is a whisper in your ear, a gaze that lingers too long, a love that refuses to die.

Whether you are new to the tale or returning to it with deeper insight, this modern translation offers a chance to rediscover one of the most evocative and daring works of gothic fiction. In its pages, you will find not just a story of the undead, but a mirror to the living—a mirror that reflects our fears, our desires, and the eternal question of what lies beneath the surface of the self.

Prologue

Attached to the following story, Doctor Hesselius wrote a detailed note, referring to an essay he had written about the unusual topic covered in the manuscript.

In his essay, he examines the subject with his usual deep knowledge and insight, presenting his ideas in a clear and precise way. This essay will eventually become part of a larger collection of his remarkable works.

Since I am publishing this story to interest general readers, I will not interfere with the intelligent lady who tells it. After careful thought, I have decided not to summarize the doctor's reasoning or include any part of his explanation. He describes the subject as one that may reveal deep mysteries about our dual nature and what lies between.

When I first came across this manuscript, I wanted to reconnect with the person who had originally shared the story with Doctor Hesselius all those years ago. Sadly, I discovered that she had passed away in the meantime.

However, I believe that her account, as told in the pages ahead, is already as detailed and truthful as anyone could expect.

Chapter I
An Early Fright

In Styria, my family and I live in a castle, or schloss, though we are not wealthy. Here, a modest income stretches much further than it would elsewhere. Even eight or nine hundred pounds a year allows for a comfortable life. Back in England, such an income might not have been enough among rich families, but in this simple, quiet place, I can't see how more money would make much of a difference to our way of living.

My father is English, though I have never been to England myself. He once served in the Austrian military but later retired with a pension and some inherited wealth. With that, he purchased this old castle and the small estate it sits on—he got it for a bargain.

It is a beautiful yet isolated place. The castle stands on a small hill, deep in a forest. A narrow, ancient road runs past the front, crossing a drawbridge that, in my lifetime, has never been raised. The moat is filled with perch and is home to many swans, their white feathers reflecting in the still water, which is also dotted with water lilies.

From a distance, the castle's grand front stands out, with its tall windows, stone towers, and Gothic chapel. In front of the gates, the forest clears into an open glade, and to the right, a steep Gothic bridge spans a dark, winding stream that disappears into the trees.

I have said this place is lonely, and that is no exaggeration. Standing at our hall door and looking toward the road, you would see that the forest stretches fifteen miles to the right and twelve to the left. The nearest village with people living in it is seven miles away, and the closest occupied castle with any history is nearly twenty miles in the other direction.

I say "inhabited village" because, just three miles west, there is a ruined town with a roofless old church. Inside, in the aisle, lie the crumbling tombs of the Karnstein family, who once ruled over this land. Their grand château, now abandoned, stands deep in the forest, looking down over the silent ruins of the village they once controlled.

As for why the town was abandoned, there is a legend—but I will tell that another time.

For now, I must explain just how few people live in our castle. Of course, I don't count the servants or those who stay in the side buildings.

The household consists of just my father and me. At the time of this story, I was only nineteen, though now eight years have passed since then.

My mother, a woman from Styria, passed away when I was a baby, so I never even remembered her. But I was raised by a kind governess who had been with me for as long as I could remember.

Her name was Madame Perrodon, a woman from Berne, and she took care of me as best as she could, making up for the mother I never knew. She was plump and kind, and her gentle presence was always a part of my life. She was always there at our small family dinners.

The fourth member of our household was Mademoiselle De Lafontaine, a "finishing governess." She was meant to refine my education. Madame Perrodon spoke French and broken English, while Mademoiselle De Lafontaine spoke both French and German. My father and I spoke English every day—not just to keep it from being forgotten, but out of patriotism.

The result? A household full of mixed languages, where visitors often laughed at the confusion! I will spare you the trouble of recreating such chaos in this story.

Occasionally, I had a few young lady friends who visited for short stays, and I sometimes returned the visits. These friendships were my main source of social life.

Of course, we received the occasional visit from neighbors—though in this part of the world, a "neighbor" might live five or six leagues away.

Still, I can assure you, my life was often lonely.

My governesses had some influence over me, but only as much as you might expect for a spoiled girl, whose only parent allowed her to do pretty much whatever she wanted.

The first event in my life that truly scared me happened when I was very young—so young that it is one of my earliest memories. Some people might think it was too small to even mention, but as you will see, it was something I could never forget.

My bedroom, which we called the nursery, was a large room on the top floor of our castle. It had a high oak ceiling, and I had the room all to myself. I was about six years old when, one night, I woke up and looked around, only to realize that my nurse and the nursery maid were gone. I thought I was completely alone.

I wasn't scared. I had never been told ghost stories or fairy tales that might have made me afraid of shadows or strange noises in the night. But I was upset. I felt abandoned and was about to start crying when I noticed something that made me stop.

A young woman's face was watching me from beside my bed. She had a calm, beautiful expression and was kneeling with her hands under my blanket. I looked at her in surprise but not in fear. She gently touched me, smiled, and then lay beside me, pulling me close. Her touch was soothing, and I felt safe. I quickly fell asleep again.

Then, I woke up suddenly to a sharp pain—like two needles had stabbed into my chest. I screamed. The woman jerked away and stared at me with wide eyes before slipping down to the floor and, as I thought, hiding under the bed.

For the first time, I was truly afraid. I screamed as loudly as I could. Within moments, my nurse, the nursery maid, and the housekeeper came rushing in. I told them what had happened, but they brushed it off, trying to calm me down.

Even though they acted normal, I could tell that something was wrong. Their faces were pale, and they looked nervous. I watched as they searched the room, looking under the bed, behind tables, and inside cupboards. I even heard the housekeeper whisper to the nurse, "Feel that spot on the bed—someone was lying there. It's still warm."

The nursery maid comforted me while they all examined my chest, where I said I had felt the pain. They checked carefully, but there were no marks to be seen.

That night, the housekeeper and the other servants stayed awake in the nursery. And from that moment on, a servant was always present in my room at night—until I was fourteen years old.

For a long time after that, I was nervous. A doctor was called to check on me. He was pale, old, and had smallpox scars on his face. I remember his long, serious face and chestnut-colored wig. He visited every two days, bringing medicine—which, of course, I hated.

The morning after I saw the mysterious woman, I was so terrified that I refused to be left alone—even though it was broad daylight.

I remember my father coming to my room, smiling and trying to cheer me up. He joked with the nurse, laughed loudly at one of her answers, and then patted my shoulder, kissed me, and told me not to be scared. He said it was just a dream and that dreams couldn't hurt me.

But I wasn't comforted. I knew it wasn't a dream. And I was still terrified.

Later, the nursery maid tried to convince me that she had been the one by my bed—that she had checked on me, lay down for a moment, and that I must have been half-asleep and mistaken her for someone else. The nurse backed up her story, but I still didn't believe it.

That same day, an elderly man wearing a long black robe came into my room with the nurse and housekeeper. He had a gentle face and spoke kindly to me. He told me they were going to pray. Then, he took my hands and asked me to softly repeat a prayer:

"Lord, hear all good prayers for us, for Jesus' sake."

I remember these words clearly because I repeated them often. For years, my nurse made me say them as part of my prayers.

I will never forget the kind old man, standing in my shadowy bedroom, with its massive, centuries-old furniture and the dim light filtering through the small windows.

He knelt down with the three women, and they prayed together. His voice was earnest but shaky, and the prayer seemed to go on forever.

I don't remember anything that happened before this event, and my memories afterward are unclear for a while. But this moment—the woman by my bed, the fear I felt, and the prayers that followed—

remains sharp in my mind, like a single bright picture surrounded by shadows.

Chapter II
A Guest

What I am about to tell you is so strange that you may find it hard to believe, but I promise you, it is completely true. I saw it with my own eyes.

It was a warm summer evening, and my father invited me to take a walk with him along the beautiful forest path in front of our home, as he sometimes did.

"General Spielsdorf won't be visiting as soon as I had hoped," my father said as we walked.

We had been expecting him to stay with us for a few weeks, and he was supposed to arrive the next day. He was bringing his niece, Mademoiselle Rheinfeldt, a girl I had never met but had heard was very charming. I had been looking forward to her visit for weeks and imagined we would spend many happy days together.

"How soon will he come, then?" I asked.

"Not until autumn—maybe in two months," he answered. "And now, my dear, I'm actually glad you never got the chance to meet Mademoiselle Rheinfeldt."

"Why?" I asked, both curious and disappointed.

"Because, my dear, she has passed away," he said. "I forgot to tell you earlier, but you weren't in the room when I received the General's letter tonight."

I was shocked. The General had written to us six or seven weeks ago, saying she wasn't feeling well, but there was nothing to suggest that she was in danger.

"Here, you can read his letter," my father said, handing it to me. "I think he is deeply grieving. His words seem written in complete distress."

We sat on a simple wooden bench under the shade of tall lime trees. The sun was setting behind the trees, filling the sky with warm, golden light. The river beside our home, which flows under the steep old bridge I mentioned before, reflected the sky's fading colors as it wound through the landscape.

I read the letter twice—once to myself and again out loud to my father—but I still couldn't fully understand it. It was full of strong emotions, and some parts didn't seem to make sense. The General's words were filled with sorrow and anger, almost as if his grief had clouded his mind.

He wrote:

"I have lost my precious child—because that's what she was to me. I loved her like my own daughter. I was unable to write to you in the final days of dear Bertha's illness. Before then, I had no idea how serious it was. Now, I have lost her, and I have learned the truth too late. She died innocent, never realizing what caused her suffering, and she left this world with faith and hope for a better one.

The wicked creature who deceived us and took advantage of our kindness is to blame for everything. I thought I was welcoming a kind, cheerful companion into our home for Bertha. But I was a fool!

Thank God, my child never suspected the true reason for her illness. She died without ever knowing the evil that had caused her pain. But I know the truth now, and I will dedicate the rest of my life to hunting down and destroying this monster.

I have been told that I may have a chance of succeeding in my mission, but right now, I have nothing to guide me. I curse my own arrogance, my blindness, my foolishness—all too late.

I cannot think clearly right now—I am overwhelmed. But once I have regained some strength, I will begin my search. I may even have to go as far as Vienna. Sometime in the autumn, two months from now—perhaps sooner, if I survive—I will visit you, if you will allow me. Then, I will tell you everything that I cannot bring myself to put into words now.

Pray for me, dear friend."

The letter ended with those words. Even though I had never met Bertha Rheinfeldt, I felt tears well up in my eyes when I learned of her sudden death. I was shaken, and I couldn't help but feel deeply disappointed.

By the time I handed the letter back to my father, the sun had set, and the sky had darkened into twilight.

It was a clear, peaceful evening, and we walked slowly, talking about what the letter could mean. The General's words were so intense and confusing that we couldn't make sense of them. We had nearly a mile to go before we reached the road in front of our home, and by the time we got there, the moon was shining brightly.

At the drawbridge, we met Madame Perrodon and Mademoiselle De Lafontaine, who had come outside without their bonnets to enjoy the moonlight. As we got closer, we could hear them talking excitedly. We joined them at the bridge and turned to admire the beautiful scenery with them.

The path we had just walked stretched out before us. To the left, the narrow road disappeared into the thick forest, winding under tall trees. To the right, the same road crossed the steep old bridge near a ruined tower that once stood guard over the area. Beyond the bridge, a rocky hill rose, covered in trees and ivy-covered stones that appeared gray in the moonlight.

A thin mist was settling over the grass and lowlands like a soft veil, making everything look distant and dreamy. Here and there, we could see the river faintly shining under the moon.

No place could have looked more calm and beautiful. The news I had just heard made me sad, but nothing could take away the peacefulness and quiet magic of the scene.

My father, who always appreciated beautiful sights, and I stood there silently, taking it all in. Behind us, the two governesses spoke about the lovely night and how bright the moon was.

Madame Perrodon was a plump, middle-aged woman with a romantic nature. She often spoke in poetic sighs and dramatic expressions. Mademoiselle De Lafontaine, on the other hand, believed she had deep psychological insight because her father was German. She had a habit of discussing mystical and philosophical ideas and now claimed that when the moon shone as brightly as it did that night, it was a sign of heightened spiritual activity.

She explained that the full moon, when so brilliant, had many effects—it influenced dreams, affected the mentally unstable, disturbed nervous people, and had strange physical effects on life itself. She even shared a story about her cousin, a sailor, who once took a nap on the deck of his ship on a night just like this. He had slept with his face exposed to the moonlight and dreamed of an old woman clawing at his cheek. When he woke up, his face was strangely twisted to one side, and it never fully returned to normal.

"The moon tonight," she said, "is filled with a magical energy. Just look at the front of the schloss behind us—see how the windows shimmer and glow as if unseen hands had lit them up, preparing the rooms for fairy guests."

There are times when we don't feel like talking but enjoy listening to the voices of others. This was one of those moments for me. I gazed at the beautiful scene, letting their conversation flow around me like soft music.

After a while, my father, who had been quiet, finally spoke. "I'm feeling strangely restless tonight," he admitted. Then, quoting Shakespeare—whom he often read aloud to keep up our English—he said:

"'In truth, I know not why I am so sad.
It wearies me; you say it wearies you;
But how I got it—came by it...'"

He paused. "I forget the rest. But I feel as if some great misfortune is hanging over us. Maybe it's the General's troubling letter that has unsettled me."

Just then, we heard an unusual sound—carriage wheels and the pounding of multiple horses on the road.

The noise grew louder as the carriage approached from the high ground beyond the bridge. Soon, we saw it emerge—a grand traveling coach, likely belonging to a person of high status. Two riders led the way, followed by the carriage pulled by four horses, with two more riders following behind.

This was a rare sight, and we were all drawn in, watching with interest. But in an instant, the scene turned from fascinating to terrifying.

As the carriage reached the top of the steep bridge, one of the lead horses panicked. Its fear spread to the others, and suddenly, the whole team bolted, breaking into a wild, uncontrollable gallop. The horses charged past the front riders and thundered toward us like a raging storm.

Our alarm grew even greater when we heard a woman's long, piercing screams coming from the carriage window.

We rushed forward, a mix of curiosity and fear gripping us. I kept silent, but the others gasped and shouted in panic.

The terrifying moment didn't last long. Just before the carriage reached the castle drawbridge, it swerved violently. To one side of the road stood a massive lime tree; on the other, an old stone cross. The horses, galloping at a terrifying speed, veered toward the tree, and one of the wheels struck its thick roots.

I knew what was about to happen. Unable to watch, I covered my eyes and turned away. At that very moment, I heard the cries of my companions, who had stepped ahead.

When I finally dared to look, I saw chaos. Two of the horses had collapsed, the carriage was on its side with two wheels in the air, and the men were frantically working to untangle the harnesses.

A tall woman with an air of authority had stepped out of the wreck, her hands clasped together. She repeatedly lifted a handkerchief to her face, as if trying to hold back her emotions.

Then, the carriage door opened, and the men carefully lifted out a young woman who appeared completely unconscious.

My dear father was already beside the older woman, his hat in hand, offering his help and inviting them to the schloss. However, she hardly seemed to hear him—her eyes were fixed only on the pale, limp girl being laid gently against the grassy slope.

I stepped closer and saw that the young woman was unconscious but alive. My father, who prided himself on having some medical knowledge, checked her pulse. He turned to the woman, who had introduced herself as the girl's mother, and assured her, "Her pulse is weak and irregular, but it's there. She's alive."

At these words, the woman clasped her hands together and looked up, as if overcome with gratitude. But almost immediately, she became emotional again, her dramatic reaction making me wonder if this was simply her natural way of expressing herself.

She was what some might call a striking woman, even at her age. She was tall, not too thin, and wore a rich black velvet dress. Her face, though pale, had a strong and noble look, but now it was full of deep distress.

As I approached, I heard the woman exclaim with clasped hands, "Who has ever been so unlucky as me? I am on a journey that is a matter of life and death, where even losing an hour could cost everything. My child won't be well enough to travel for who knows how long. I have no choice but to leave her behind—I cannot wait. How far is the nearest village, sir? I must leave her there, and I won't see or hear from my beloved daughter for three months until I return."

I tugged at my father's coat and whispered urgently, "Oh, Papa, please ask her to let the girl stay with us—it would be wonderful! Please, ask her."

My father turned to the lady and said, "Madame, if you would entrust your daughter to my care, along with my own daughter and her kind governess, Madame Perrodon, we would be honored to have her as our guest. We would care for her with all the attention and kindness she deserves until your return."

The woman shook her head anxiously. "I cannot do that, sir. It would be asking too much of your kindness."

"Not at all," my father assured her. "In fact, you would be doing us a great favor. My daughter was recently disappointed by a canceled visit she had been looking forward to for so long. Having your daughter here would be the best way to cheer her up. The nearest village on your route is quite far, and there isn't a proper inn where you could comfortably leave her. You also cannot risk continuing your journey with her in this condition. If you truly must leave tonight, there is no better or safer place for her than here."

There was something about this lady—her appearance, her noble manner—that made it clear she was a woman of high status, even apart from the grand carriage she traveled in.

By now, the coach had been lifted upright, and the horses, now calm, were harnessed again and ready to go.

The lady cast a quick glance at her daughter—one that, strangely, did not seem as warm or loving as I would have expected. Then she signaled to my father, stepping a few feet away to speak with him privately. Her expression changed completely—now serious, even stern, unlike the emotional way she had spoken earlier.

I was amazed that my father didn't seem to notice the sudden change in her tone. More than anything, I was desperate to know what she was saying to him in such a quiet, urgent manner.

After only a few minutes, she turned back toward her daughter, who was being supported by Madame Perrodon. Kneeling beside the girl, she whispered something—Madame Perrodon later guessed it was a short blessing. Then, with a quick kiss, she rose to her feet and hurried to the carriage.

The door shut behind her, and the uniformed footmen jumped onto the back. The lead riders spurred their horses forward, the postilions cracked their whips, and the horses lunged ahead, suddenly breaking into a furious pace that looked as though it might turn into another wild gallop. The carriage sped away, disappearing into the night, followed closely by the two men on horseback.

Chapter III
We Compare Notes

We watched the carriage and its riders disappear into the misty forest until even the sound of the wheels and hooves had faded into the quiet night. The only proof that it had all really happened was the young lady who, at that moment, slowly opened her eyes.

I couldn't see her face since she was turned away from me, but she lifted her head and, in a soft and sweet voice, asked, "Where is my mother?"

Madame Perrodon spoke to her gently, offering words of comfort.

Then the girl asked, "Where am I? What is this place?" After a pause, she added, "I don't see the carriage… and Matska, where is she?"

Madame Perrodon did her best to answer her questions, and slowly, the young lady seemed to remember what had happened. She was relieved to hear that no one had been hurt but became tearful when she learned that her mother had left her behind and wouldn't return for three months.

I was about to offer my own words of comfort when Mademoiselle De Lafontaine touched my arm and whispered, "Don't overwhelm her. She can only handle talking to one person at a time right now. Too much excitement could be bad for her."

I decided I would visit her later once she was settled in her room.

Meanwhile, my father had sent a servant on horseback to fetch a doctor who lived about two leagues away. A bedroom was also being prepared for the young lady's stay.

She stood up slowly, leaning on Madame Perrodon's arm as they walked across the drawbridge and into the castle. Inside the hall, servants waited to greet her and immediately led her to her room.

The room where we usually spent our evenings was long, with four windows overlooking the moat and the forest beyond. It was furnished with dark, carved oak, grand cabinets, and chairs covered in deep red velvet. Tapestries hung on the walls, depicting life-sized figures in old-fashioned clothing, engaged in hunting and feasting. Although it looked formal, the room was still warm and inviting. My father, always loyal to English traditions, insisted that tea be served along with our usual coffee and chocolate.

That night, we gathered in that room, the candlelight flickering as we discussed the strange events of the evening.

Madame Perrodon and Mademoiselle De Lafontaine had joined us, as the young stranger had fallen into a deep sleep shortly after being placed in bed. A servant remained to watch over her.

"What do you think of our guest?" I asked eagerly once Madame Perrodon entered. "Tell me everything about her."

"I like her very much," she replied. "She might be the prettiest girl I've ever seen—about your age, and so kind and delicate."

"She's absolutely beautiful," Mademoiselle De Lafontaine added, having taken a quick peek into the girl's room.

"And her voice is lovely," Madame Perrodon said.

Then Mademoiselle De Lafontaine asked, "Did you notice the woman who stayed in the carriage after it was upright again? She never got out, only looked at us through the window."

None of us had seen her, so she described the woman—a frightening-looking figure with dark skin, wearing a brightly colored turban. She had been watching them with wide, gleaming eyes, grinning strangely, and nodding toward them in a way that seemed mocking or even angry.

"Did you notice how rough and suspicious the servants looked?" Madame Perrodon asked.

"Yes," my father replied as he walked into the room. "They were some of the most unpleasant-looking men I've ever seen. I just hope they don't turn on that poor woman and rob her in the forest. Though I must admit, they were quick to get everything back in order."

"They're probably just exhausted from too much traveling," Madame suggested.

"Even so, their faces looked so gaunt, dark, and unfriendly," she continued. "I can't help but be curious. But I suppose the young lady will tell us more tomorrow if she's feeling better."

"I don't think she will," my father said with a knowing smile. He gave a small nod, as if he understood something we didn't.

That only made us more eager to know what had happened in the brief but intense conversation between him and the lady in black velvet before she left.

Once we were alone, I begged him to tell me. It didn't take much persuasion.

"There's no real reason not to tell you," my father said. "She didn't want to burden us with her daughter's care, saying the girl was in delicate health and easily frightened, but not prone to seizures—she made sure to mention that—or to any delusions. In fact, she said she was perfectly sane."

"That's such a strange thing to say," I interrupted. "It wasn't necessary at all."

"Maybe not, but she said it," he chuckled. "And since you want to hear everything, which honestly wasn't much, I'm telling you. She also said, 'I am on an extremely important journey'—she really stressed that part—'It must be fast and kept secret. I will return in three months. Until then, my daughter will not speak about who we are, where we are from, or where we are going.' That's all she told me. Her French was perfect. But when she said 'secret,' she paused for a few seconds and gave me a very serious look. I think that part really mattered to her. And you saw how quickly she left. I just hope I wasn't foolish to take the girl in."

I, on the other hand, was thrilled. I couldn't wait to meet her and talk to her, but I had to wait for the doctor's approval. If you've always lived in a busy town, you can't imagine how exciting it is to meet a new friend in a place as isolated as ours.

The doctor didn't arrive until nearly one o'clock. But there was no way I could have gone to bed and fallen asleep—I would have had better luck chasing down the mysterious woman's carriage on foot.

When the doctor finally came downstairs, he gave a very positive report. His patient was sitting up, her pulse was steady, and she seemed perfectly fine. There was no sign of injury, and the little shock she'd suffered had passed without any real harm. He said there was no reason I couldn't visit her if we both wanted to.

With that, I immediately sent a message to ask if she would allow me to come see her.

The servant returned right away with her answer—she would love nothing more.

I didn't waste a moment.

She was resting in one of the grandest rooms in the castle. It was a bit formal, with dark, old tapestries hanging on the walls. One directly across from the bed showed Cleopatra holding a pair of asps to her chest. Other faded images of classical figures decorated the room. But despite this, there was enough gold detailing and rich colors in the rest of the décor to keep it from feeling too gloomy.

Candles were glowing at her bedside. She was sitting up, her delicate figure wrapped in a silk dressing gown embroidered with flowers. The thick, quilted fabric had been placed over her by her mother when she lay on the ground earlier.

But as I reached her bedside and began to greet her, I suddenly stopped. My words froze in my throat, and I instinctively took a step back.

I knew that face.

It was the very same face that had appeared in my childhood. The one that haunted my dreams for years. The face I had thought about in secret, filled with fear, while everyone else remained unaware.

She was beautiful, just as I remembered, with the same sorrowful expression as before.

But then, just as suddenly, her face changed.

A strange, knowing smile spread across her lips.

We stared at each other in silence for a full minute before she finally spoke. I couldn't.

"How incredible," she said softly. "Twelve years ago, I saw your face in a dream. I've never forgotten it."

"Incredible indeed," I echoed, forcing myself to push past the shock that had stolen my voice. "Twelve years ago, whether in a dream or real life, I know I saw you too. I could never forget your face. It has stayed in my mind ever since."

Her expression softened. The oddness I had seen in her smile faded, and now she simply looked kind and lovely, her cheeks dimpling as she smiled again.

Feeling reassured, I quickly shifted my tone to one of warmth, as any good host should. I told her how happy we all were to have her here and how much I personally welcomed her arrival.

I took her hand as I spoke. Being a rather shy person—something that often happens when you live a quiet life—I felt a little nervous. But the moment made me braver than usual. She pressed my hand, then placed hers over mine, her eyes meeting mine with an intense glow. She smiled again, her cheeks turning pink.

She responded to my welcome so sweetly. I sat beside her, still trying to understand it all, and she said:

"I have to tell you about my dream of you. It's so strange that we both had such vivid dreams of each other, that we saw each other exactly as we are now, even though we were just little children at the time. I was around six years old when I woke up from a confusing and unsettling dream. I found myself in a room that didn't look like my nursery at all. The walls were covered in dark wood, and there were cupboards, beds, chairs, and benches scattered around. I thought all the beds were empty, and I didn't see anyone else in the room except for myself.

After looking around for a while, I noticed an iron candlestick with two branches that caught my eye—I know I would recognize it if I saw it again. Then, I crawled under one of the beds to get closer to the window. But just as I was getting out from underneath, I heard someone crying. I looked up while still on my knees, and I saw you— without a doubt, it was you, exactly as I see you now. A beautiful young girl with golden hair, big blue eyes, and lips that look just like yours.

There was something about you that made me feel safe. I climbed onto the bed and wrapped my arms around you. I think we both fell asleep. But then, I was suddenly woken up by a scream—you were sitting up and crying out. I got scared and slid off the bed. It felt like I passed out for a moment, and when I woke up again, I was back in my nursery at home. But I never forgot your face. It wasn't just a coincidence or a resemblance. You are the girl I saw that night."

Now it was my turn to tell her about my own dream, and as I did, she listened with wide-eyed amazement.

"I don't know which one of us should be more afraid of the other," she said with a teasing smile. "If you weren't so lovely, I think I'd be quite frightened of you. But since you are—and since we're both still young—I feel as if we met twelve years ago and already share a special connection. It seems like we were meant to be friends from the start. Do you feel the same pull toward me as I do toward you? I've never had a real friend—do you think I might finally find one now?"

She sighed, and her deep, dark eyes looked at me with a kind of intensity I had never seen before.

The truth is, I felt something strange toward her. I was drawn to her, just as she said, but at the same time, there was something unsettling about it. Still, my fascination with her overpowered any hesitation. She was captivating, both in her beauty and the way she spoke.

I noticed that she was beginning to look tired, so I quickly said good night.

"The doctor thinks you should have someone stay with you tonight," I told her. "One of our maids is waiting outside. She's very quiet and will be helpful if you need anything."

She smiled kindly. "That's so thoughtful of you, but I really can't sleep with someone else in the room. I never could. I don't need any help—though, should I admit my little fear? I've always been terrified of robbers. Once, my home was broken into, and two servants were killed. Ever since then, I always lock my door at night. It's just a habit now. And you're so sweet—I know you'll understand. I see there's a key in the lock."

She pulled me into a quick hug, holding me close for a moment before whispering, "Good night, darling. It's so hard to say goodbye, but good night. I'll see you again tomorrow—but not too early."

She lay back on the pillow with a sigh, her beautiful eyes following me as I stepped away. They were warm but sad. As I left, I heard her murmur once more, "Good night, dear friend."

Young people tend to form attachments quickly. I couldn't help but feel flattered by the affection she showed me, even though I hadn't done anything to earn it yet. I liked how she welcomed me so easily. It was clear that she had already decided we were going to be close friends.

The next day, we met again. In many ways, I was completely charmed by her.

In the daylight, her beauty was even more striking—she was, without a doubt, the most beautiful person I had ever seen. And the unsettling memory of her face from my childhood dream no longer had the same eerie effect on me.

She admitted that she had felt a similar shock when she first saw me and had experienced the same odd mix of fascination and unease.

We laughed together at how silly our initial fears seemed now.

Chapter IV
Her Habits—A Saunter

I told you before that I was enchanted by her in many ways. But there were also things about her that I didn't quite like.

First, let me describe her. She was taller than most women, very slim, and incredibly graceful. The only thing that hinted at weakness was the way she moved—slowly, almost lazily. Otherwise, she looked completely healthy. Her skin was glowing and full of color, her features were delicate and perfectly shaped, and her large, dark eyes were full of life. But the most striking thing about her was her hair—it was the thickest and longest I had ever seen. When she let it down, it flowed past her shoulders, and I often played with it, marveling at its softness and weight. It was a deep brown with golden highlights, so fine and silky that I loved running my fingers through it as we talked. If only I had known the truth back then!

But as much as I liked her, there were things that bothered me. From the very first night, her openness and warmth had made me feel close to her. Yet at the same time, she was incredibly secretive about herself. She never spoke about her mother, her past, or even the simplest details of her life—where she was from, where she was going, or who her family was. Maybe I was wrong to push for answers, and perhaps I should have respected the promise my father made to her mother. But my curiosity was too strong. Why wouldn't she trust me? Did she think I wasn't worthy of her secrets? I swore to her, over and over, that I would never repeat anything she told me, yet she still refused to share even the smallest detail.

She wasn't cold or unkind about it. In fact, she smiled gently every time she refused to answer. But I felt that her silence was unnatural for someone so young. We never fought about it because she wouldn't argue. I knew I was being unfair to keep asking, but I just couldn't stop myself. Still, no matter how much I begged, I got nowhere.

The only things she ever told me were three vague facts:

1. Her name was Carmilla.

2. Her family was very old and noble.

3. Her home was somewhere in the west.

She wouldn't tell me her last name, her family's coat of arms, the name of their estate, or even what country she was from.

It wasn't that I asked her constantly. I tried to bring it up casually, hoping she might share something without realizing it. Sometimes, I asked her directly. No matter what approach I took, I always failed. Neither pleading nor teasing worked. But even when she refused, she did it in such a sweet and sorrowful way that I couldn't stay upset for long. She would wrap her arms around me, press her cheek to mine, and whisper,

"My dear, I know this upsets you. Please don't think I'm being unkind—I have no choice. If your heart hurts, mine does too. I feel alive because of you, and one day, you will become a part of me. I can't change it. And one day, just like I'm drawn to you, you will be drawn to others. You'll understand the kind of love that also holds a bit of cruelty. For now, don't try to figure it out—just trust me."

Then she would hold me tighter, her body trembling, and softly kiss my cheek.

Her words confused me. They made no sense, yet there was something hypnotic about them.

She didn't always act like this, but when she did, I wanted to pull away. And yet, I couldn't. It was as if my strength left me, and I felt trapped in a dream. Her voice was like a lullaby, making it impossible to resist. I would only come back to my senses when she finally let go.

When she was in these strange moods, I didn't like her. I felt restless, caught between emotions I didn't understand. There was excitement, and even a kind of pleasure, but underneath it all, I felt an uneasy fear. My thoughts were unclear, but I knew one thing—my feelings for her were growing stronger, even turning into devotion. And yet, at the same time, I felt a deep and terrible sense of dread.

It makes no sense, I know. But that's the only way I can describe it.

It has been more than ten years since these events, and as I write now, my hands tremble. My memories of certain moments are blurry and frightening, yet the main events remain sharp in my mind.

I believe that in every life, there are moments when emotions run so wild and intense that later, they become difficult to recall clearly.

Sometimes, after sitting in silence for a long time, my strange but beautiful companion would suddenly take my hand and squeeze it affectionately, over and over again. She would blush softly, her deep, burning eyes fixed on mine, and her breathing would quicken so much that I could see her chest rise and fall. The way she looked at me was like that of someone in love. It made me uncomfortable, even frightened, yet I couldn't pull away. With a longing look, she would draw me close, her warm lips brushing my cheek with kisses. Then, in a whisper, almost like a sob, she would say, "You are mine. You will always be mine. We are one forever." And suddenly, she would pull away, covering her eyes with her hands, leaving me shaking.

"Are we related?" I would ask, confused. "What do you mean by all this? Do I remind you of someone you loved? You have to stop— I don't like it! I don't even know you, and I don't know myself when you act this way!"

At my outburst, she would sigh and let go of my hand, turning away.

I tried to make sense of these strange moments, but no explanation seemed to fit. She wasn't playing a trick—it felt too real, too sudden, like something deep inside her was bursting out. Was she experiencing brief moments of madness, despite her mother's claims that she was perfectly sane? Or was this some kind of disguise, a strange story unfolding in real life? I had read old books about such things—about young men sneaking into houses in disguise, aided by clever older women. But that idea didn't quite fit.

Outside of these passionate moments, she was different. Sometimes she was cheerful, other times distant and quiet, watching me with sad, intense eyes. There were long stretches of time when she barely seemed to notice me. And despite her sudden bursts of affection, she never showed the kind of interest a man might when trying to win a woman's heart.

Her daily habits were unusual—maybe not so strange for someone from a city, but to us, living in the countryside, they seemed odd. She slept late and rarely came downstairs before one in the afternoon. She would drink a cup of chocolate but eat nothing, then go for a walk with me. Yet she would tire quickly, sometimes so much that she needed to rest on a bench under the trees or return to the house. Though her body seemed weak, her mind was full of energy—she talked a lot, and she was always fascinating to listen to.

Now and then, she would mention something about her home, a story from her past, or describe people with customs completely unfamiliar to me. From these little hints, I began to realize that her home must have been much farther away than I had first thought.

One afternoon, we were sitting under the trees when a funeral procession passed by. It was for a young girl I had often seen before— the daughter of a forest ranger. Her father walked behind the coffin, his face full of grief. She had been his only child.

Behind him, villagers walked in pairs, singing a funeral hymn.

Out of respect, I stood up and joined in the song, my heart heavy for the poor father.

But then, I felt my companion grab my arm roughly. Startled, I turned to her in surprise.

She suddenly said, "Don't you hear how awful that sounds?"

"I think it's actually very sweet," I replied, annoyed that she had interrupted me and worried that the people in the procession might notice and take offense.

I started singing again, but she quickly stopped me. "You're hurting my ears," Carmilla said almost angrily, covering them with her small hands. "Besides, how do you even know that we share the same beliefs? Your traditions upset me, and I hate funerals. What's the point? Everyone has to die—there's no avoiding it. And when they do, they're better off. Let's go home."

"My father went with the priest to the graveyard," I explained. "Didn't you know the girl was being buried today?"

"She?" Carmilla scoffed. "I don't care about peasants. I don't even know who she was."

"She was the poor girl who thought she saw a ghost two weeks ago. She had been slowly dying ever since, and yesterday, she finally passed away."

"Don't talk about ghosts! I won't be able to sleep if you do," she insisted.

"I just hope it's not some kind of disease," I went on. "It's starting to seem like one. The swineherd's young wife died just last week. She said she felt something grab her by the throat in the middle of the night, as if it was choking her. Papa says fevers can cause people to imagine terrible things like that. She had been fine the day before, but after that night, she got weaker and weaker until she died."

"Well, at least her funeral is over, and her awful song is done," Carmilla muttered. "That noise was unbearable. It made me feel sick. Sit with me—sit close. Hold my hand, and press it hard. Harder!"

We had stepped away from the road and found another bench. She sat down, but then something strange happened. Her face suddenly changed—it became pale and dark at the same time, almost ashen. Her hands clenched into fists, and her teeth pressed tightly together. Her whole body trembled as if she was fighting off an attack, her lips pressed together as she stared at the ground. A deep shudder ran through her, and finally, a small, pained cry escaped her lips. Slowly, whatever had taken over her seemed to fade.

"There! That's what happens when people strangle others with their hymns," she finally said. "Hold me. Keep holding me. It's passing."

Gradually, her body relaxed, and, as if to distract from what had just happened, she suddenly became unusually talkative and cheerful. We made our way home, and I tried to push aside the uneasy feeling left in me.

This was the first time I had seen any real signs of weakness in her health, which her mother had once mentioned. It was also the first time I saw her get truly irritated or upset. Both feelings passed quickly, like a summer cloud, and after that, I only saw her angry once more.

It happened when we were looking out of the large drawing room windows. A familiar figure entered the courtyard, crossing over the drawbridge. He was a wandering entertainer who visited twice a year.

He was a hunchback, with sharp, thin features often seen in people with his condition. He had a pointed black beard and a wide, toothy grin. He wore a mix of buff, black, and red clothing, covered in so many belts and straps that I lost count. From them hung all sorts of strange things.

On his back, he carried a magic lantern and two small wooden boxes. I knew them well—one held a so-called salamander, the other a mandrake. These odd creatures always made my father laugh. They were stitched together from dried parts of monkeys, parrots, squirrels, fish, and hedgehogs, creating grotesque little monsters.

He also had a fiddle, a box of magic tricks, a pair of fencing swords with masks tied to his belt, and several other mysterious objects dangling from his body. In his hand, he held a black staff with copper fittings.

His only companion was a scruffy-looking dog that followed at his heels but hesitated at the drawbridge. A few moments later, the dog began to howl.

Meanwhile, the man stepped into the courtyard, removed his strange, oversized hat, and bowed deeply with an exaggerated flourish. Then, in a jumble of terrible French and slightly better German, he introduced himself with dramatic flair.

Without missing a beat, he pulled out his fiddle and started playing a lively tune, singing along in a wild, off-key voice while dancing with silly, exaggerated movements. I couldn't help but laugh, despite the dog's eerie howling.

After his performance, he approached the window, smiling broadly. With his hat in one hand and his fiddle tucked under his arm, he launched into a breathless speech, listing all the talents he had to offer and the wonders he could show us.

The man dropped his hat to the ground and said, "Would your ladyships like to buy a charm to protect you from the oupire? I hear it's roaming these woods like a wolf. People are dying left and right, but this charm never fails. Just pin it to your pillow, and you can laugh in its face."

The charms were small, rectangular pieces of parchment covered in strange symbols and markings.

Carmilla immediately bought one, and so did I.

As we smiled down at him, amused, his sharp black eyes suddenly seemed to catch something that piqued his curiosity. Without hesitation, he unrolled a leather case filled with small, odd-looking steel tools.

"Look here, my lady," he said, directing his attention toward me. "Among my many skills, I also practice dentistry. And—curse that dog! Silence, beast!—your noble friend, the young lady beside you, has the sharpest tooth I've ever seen. Long, thin, and pointed like a needle— ha! With my keen eyesight, I spotted it immediately. Now, if it happens to bother the young lady, and I imagine it must, I can help. Here I am, with my file, my punch, and my nippers. I can smooth it out, make it round and blunt—no longer the tooth of a beast, but a proper tooth for a beautiful young lady like herself. What do you say? Is she displeased? Have I spoken too boldly? Have I offended her?"

Carmilla looked furious. She pulled back from the window, her face filled with anger.

"How dare that wretched man insult us? Where is your father? I will demand justice from him. My father would have had this scoundrel tied to a post, whipped like a common thief, and branded like cattle!"

She stepped away from the window and sat down, still fuming. But as soon as the man was out of sight, her anger faded just as quickly as it had flared up. Before long, she seemed to forget about the whole incident.

That evening, my father seemed troubled. When he returned home, he told us that another case—similar to the two recent deaths—had occurred. The sister of a young peasant on his land, only a mile away, had fallen ill. She described an attack just like the others and was now slowly wasting away.

"All of this," my father said, "has a natural explanation. These poor people are spreading their fears among each other, imagining they're experiencing the same thing as their neighbors."

"But that makes it even more terrifying," Carmilla said.

"How so?" my father asked.

"I'm afraid of imagining things myself. I feel like it would be just as bad as if it were real."

"We are in God's hands," my father assured her. "Nothing can happen without His will. Everything will be fine for those who trust in Him. He created us all and will watch over us."

"Creator? Nature," Carmilla replied with a strange tone. "And this sickness spreading through the land—isn't it just nature? Everything that happens in the sky, on the earth, and below the ground—doesn't it all come from nature? Isn't that how the world works?"

"The doctor said he would visit us today," my father said after a brief silence. "I want to hear his thoughts on this and see what he suggests we do."

"Doctors have never helped me," Carmilla muttered.

"You've been sick before?" I asked.

"Sicker than you've ever been," she replied.

"A long time ago?"

"Yes, a very long time ago. I had this very same illness. But I hardly remember anything besides the pain and weakness. And honestly, it wasn't as bad as other diseases."

"You must have been very young then."

"I suppose so. Let's not talk about it anymore. You wouldn't want to hurt a friend, would you?"

She looked at me softly, put an arm around my waist, and led me out of the room. My father was still at his desk, focused on some papers.

"Why does your father insist on scaring us?" she asked with a sigh.

"He doesn't mean to, Carmilla. That's the last thing he wants."

"Are you afraid, dear?"

"I would be, if I thought there was any real danger that I might be attacked like those poor people were."

"You're afraid of dying?"

"Yes, isn't everyone?"

"But what if you could die the way lovers do—together, so they never have to be apart? Girls are like caterpillars while they live in this world, waiting for summer to turn them into butterflies. But before that, we're just larvae and grubs, each with different needs, different instincts. That's what Monsieur Buffon says in his big book in the next room."

Later that day, the doctor arrived and had a long private conversation with my father.

He was an experienced man, well past sixty, with powdered hair and a smooth, pale face. When he and my father finally came out of the study, I overheard my father laughing as he spoke.

"Well, I'm surprised at a wise man like you! Next, you'll be telling me you believe in hippogriffs and dragons."

The doctor smiled and shook his head. "Still, life and death are full of mysteries, and we know very little about the forces at work in both."

With that, they walked away, and I didn't hear any more of their conversation. At the time, I didn't know what the doctor had suggested. But looking back now, I think I can guess.

Chapter V
A Wonderful Likeness

That evening, a young man with a serious face arrived from Gratz, bringing a horse and cart loaded with two large wooden crates filled with paintings. The journey had been long—about ten leagues—and whenever someone came from the town, we all gathered excitedly in the hall to hear any news.

This visit caused quite a stir in our quiet home. The crates were left in the hall, while the young man was taken care of by the servants and given supper. Once he had eaten, he and a few helpers returned, carrying tools like hammers and chisels, ready to open the cases. We all stood around, eager to see the paintings inside.

Carmilla sat nearby, watching with little interest as the old portraits were carefully revealed, one by one. Most of them had been in our family for generations, passed down from my mother's Hungarian relatives. My father held a list in his hand, checking off each painting as the young man unpacked them. They were not necessarily great works of art, but they were certainly very old, and many were fascinating to look at. Since they had been covered in dust and smoke for so long, it felt like I was seeing them for the first time.

"There is one painting I haven't seen yet," my father said. "There's a name written on it—at least, as far as I could make it out before it was cleaned. 'Marcia Karnstein' and the date '1698.' I'm curious to see how it looks now."

I remembered the painting. It was small, about a foot and a half high, nearly square, and had no frame. But it had been so darkened with age that I had never been able to see it clearly.

Now, the young man brought it out, obviously proud of his work. The difference was stunning—it was beautiful, almost lifelike. And to my complete shock, it looked exactly like Carmilla.

"Carmilla, look! This is unbelievable. It's you—alive, smiling, about to speak. Papa, isn't it incredible? Look, it even has the little mole on her throat!"

My father chuckled. "It is quite a remarkable resemblance," he admitted. But to my surprise, he didn't seem as amazed as I was. Instead, he turned his attention back to the young man, discussing the cleaning process and the other portraits, while I continued to stare in wonder at the painting.

"Papa, can I hang this in my room?" I asked.

"Of course, dear," he said, smiling. "If you think it looks so much like her, then it must be even prettier than I thought."

But Carmilla didn't respond to the compliment. She didn't seem to have even heard it. She was leaning back in her chair, watching me with dreamy eyes, a small, pleased smile on her lips.

"And now that it's been cleaned, I can read the name clearly," I said. "It's not Marcia after all—it's written in gold. The name is Mircalla, Countess Karnstein. And look, there's a little crown above it, with the year 1698 below. I'm related to the Karnsteins—on my mother's side."

Carmilla sighed. "Ah… I think I am too," she said softly. "A very distant relation. A very old family." Then she asked, "Are there any Karnsteins still alive?"

"I don't think so," I said. "I believe the family lost everything in a war long ago. But the ruins of their castle are only about three miles from here."

"How interesting," she murmured, sounding distracted. Then, as if losing interest in the topic entirely, she turned toward the hall door, which was slightly open. "Look at that beautiful moonlight," she said. "Shall we take a little walk around the courtyard and look at the road and river?"

"It's just like the night you arrived," I said.

She let out a soft sigh and smiled.

We walked outside, arm in arm, moving slowly down to the drawbridge, where the landscape stretched out before us in the silver light of the moon.

"So, you were thinking about the night I arrived?" she whispered. "Are you glad I came?"

"Of course, dear Carmilla," I answered. "I'm so happy you're here."

"And you wanted the painting that looks like me, to keep in your room," she murmured, tightening her arm around my waist and resting her head on my shoulder.

"How romantic you are, Carmilla," I said, smiling. "When you finally tell me your story, I'm sure it will be filled with one grand romance."

She kissed me softly without saying a word.

"Carmilla, I think you've been in love before," I said. "Maybe you're in love right now."

She whispered, "I have never loved anyone, and I never will—unless it's you."

In the moonlight, she looked more beautiful than ever. Then, suddenly, she buried her face in my neck and hair, letting out deep, shaky sighs, almost like quiet sobs. Her hand trembled as she held mine.

Her warm cheek pressed against mine as she murmured, "My darling, I live through you. And you would die for me, because I love you so."

I pulled away, startled.

She was staring at me, but her eyes were empty now, the fire in them gone. Her face was pale and expressionless.

"Is it colder now?" she asked drowsily. "I feel like I'm shivering… Was I dreaming? Let's go inside. Come, come inside."

"You don't look well, Carmilla. You seem a little faint," I said. "You should have some wine."

"Yes, I will. I feel better now. In a few minutes, I'll be completely fine. But yes, please, give me a little wine," she said as we reached the door. Then she paused.

"Let's stay out just a little longer," she added. "This might be the last time I see the moonlight with you."

"How are you feeling now? Are you sure you're better?" I asked, growing worried. The strange illness people had been talking about in the villages crossed my mind.

"Papa would be so upset if you were sick, even just a little," I said. "If you feel unwell, we need to tell him. There's a very good doctor nearby—he saw Papa today."

"I know how kind you all are," she said gently. "But I promise, I'm fine now. The only thing ever wrong with me is a little weakness. People say I seem tired all the time, like I don't have much energy. I can barely walk farther than a little child. And sometimes, I just suddenly lose the little strength I have, like you just saw. But it always passes quickly. Look, I'm already better."

And it was true. She looked perfectly fine again. We talked for a long time, and she was full of life and laughter. The rest of the evening passed without her saying or doing anything strange—none of the unsettling words or looks that sometimes confused and even frightened me.

But later that night, something happened that changed everything. It shifted my thoughts in a completely new direction—and even startled Carmilla out of her usual calm.

Chapter VI
A Very Strange Agony

After we returned to the drawing room, we sat down for coffee and chocolate. Carmilla didn't have any, but she seemed back to normal. Madame and Mademoiselle De Lafontaine joined us for a small card game, and soon my father came in for his usual evening tea.

When the game was over, he sat next to Carmilla on the sofa and asked if she had heard from her mother since she arrived. She simply answered, "No."

Then he asked if she knew where to send a letter to reach her.

"I don't know for sure," she said vaguely. "But I've been thinking about leaving. You've all been so kind, and I've already caused too much trouble. I'd like to take a carriage tomorrow and go find her. I know where she'll be eventually, but I can't tell you yet."

"You mustn't even think of such a thing!" my father exclaimed, which filled me with relief. "We can't let you leave so suddenly, and I won't allow it unless your mother herself comes to get you. She trusted us to care for you until she returned. I would feel much better if we heard from her soon. But for now, I take my responsibility seriously. The illness spreading in the villages has gotten even worse, and I can't risk anything happening to you. So until your mother says otherwise, you must stay here. We care about you too much to let you go so easily."

"Thank you, sir," Carmilla said sweetly. "You have all been so kind. I have rarely felt as happy as I have here in your beautiful home, with your care and your lovely daughter's company."

My father, clearly pleased with her words, smiled and kissed her hand in his old-fashioned, gentlemanly way.

As usual, I walked with Carmilla to her room and sat with her while she got ready for bed.

"Do you think you'll ever tell me everything?" I asked at last.

She turned to me, smiling but saying nothing.

"You won't answer?" I said. "Maybe I shouldn't have asked."

"No, you were right to ask," she replied. "You don't know how much you mean to me, or you wouldn't think it too much to expect my trust. But I am bound by a promise—even more strictly than a nun—and I can't tell my story just yet, not even to you. But the time is very near when you'll know everything.

"You'll think I'm selfish, and maybe I am. But love is always selfish. The stronger it is, the more selfish it becomes. You can't imagine how jealous I am. You must come with me, loving me, even to death. Or if you hate me, then hate me—but still come with me. There is no middle ground with me."

"Now you're talking nonsense again, Carmilla," I said, flustered.

"No, not nonsense," she said, shaking her head. "I may be silly and full of strange ideas, but for your sake, I'll talk sensibly. Have you ever been to a ball?"

"No. Why do you ask? It must be wonderful," I said.

"I almost forget what it's like," she murmured. "It was so long ago."

I laughed. "You're not that old! You can't have forgotten your first ball already."

"I remember it, but only if I try very hard," she said. "It's like looking through water—everything is blurry and rippling. That night, something happened that changed everything. It made my memories unclear. I was nearly killed in my sleep—stabbed here." She touched her chest lightly. "I was never the same after that."

"Were you close to dying?" I asked in shock.

"Yes. It was a cruel love... a strange love that almost took my life. Love demands sacrifices. And there is no sacrifice without blood."

She sighed. "Let's sleep now. I feel so tired. I don't even have the energy to get up and lock my door."

She lay on her pillow, her small hands buried in her thick, wavy hair. Her bright eyes followed my every move with a soft smile I couldn't quite understand.

I wished her good night and left the room with an uneasy feeling.

I often wondered if Carmilla ever said her prayers. I had never seen her kneel to pray. She never joined us for morning prayers and always slept in late. At night, she never excused herself when we gathered in the hall for a short evening prayer.

If it hadn't come up casually in one of our conversations that she had been baptized, I might have doubted that Carmilla was a Christian. She never talked about religion—not even once. If I had known more about people, I might not have been so surprised by her indifference to the subject.

Nervous habits can be contagious, and over time, I found myself copying Carmilla's precautions. Like her, I had started locking my bedroom door at night, convincing myself that I needed protection from midnight intruders and lurking dangers. I also picked up her habit of quickly checking around my room before bed, just to make sure no one was hiding inside.

Once I felt safe, I climbed into bed and quickly fell asleep. I always slept with a light on—something I had done since I was little and could never bring myself to stop. With the warm glow of my candle, I felt secure. But dreams don't care about locked doors or well-lit rooms. They slip through walls, brighten the darkness, or darken the light, moving as they please.

That night, I had a dream that haunted me in a way I had never experienced before. I wouldn't call it a nightmare because I was fully aware that I was dreaming. At the same time, I was also sure that I was in my bedroom, lying in my bed exactly as I was in real life. Everything in the room looked the same, except the space seemed much darker.

Then I noticed something moving at the foot of my bed. At first, I couldn't make out what it was, but soon I saw it clearly—a shadowy black animal, shaped like an enormous cat. It was about four or five feet long, stretching across the entire length of the hearthrug as it paced back and forth with restless energy, like a wild beast trapped in a cage.

I was terrified, but no matter how hard I tried, I couldn't scream. The creature started moving faster, and the room became even darker until the only thing I could see was its glowing eyes.

Suddenly, it leaped onto my bed.

Its large, staring eyes came closer and closer to my face. Then, out of nowhere, I felt a sharp, stabbing pain—like two long needles piercing deep into my chest.

I woke up screaming.

The room was still lit by my candle, just as I had left it. But standing at the foot of my bed, slightly to the right, was a figure dressed in a loose, dark gown. Its long hair hung down over its shoulders, and it stood completely still—so still that I couldn't even see it breathing.

As I stared in horror, the figure seemed to move slightly, shifting toward the door. Then, as if it had never been there at all, it slipped out, vanishing as the door quietly opened and shut behind it.

Suddenly, I could breathe again. I could move. But I was frozen in fear. My first thought was that Carmilla had sneaked into my room as some kind of joke. Maybe I had forgotten to lock my door.

I rushed to check—but no. The door was still locked from the inside, just as I had left it.

I was too afraid to open it. A cold dread filled my chest.

Panicking, I ran back to my bed, pulled the covers over my head, and stayed there, hardly daring to breathe. I felt more dead than alive until the morning light finally came.

Chapter VII
Descending

Even now, I can't explain the deep horror I still feel when I think about that night. It wasn't just a brief fear that faded like a bad dream. Instead, it grew stronger with time, making my room and even the furniture seem eerie, as if they held a memory of what had happened.

The next day, I couldn't stand being alone for even a moment. I thought about telling my father, but two things held me back. First, I was afraid he would laugh at me, and I couldn't bear the thought of my fear being treated as a joke. Second, I worried he might think I had caught the strange illness spreading through the area. I didn't believe I was sick, but since my father hadn't been feeling well for a while, I didn't want to worry him.

I felt safe enough with Madame Perrodon and Mademoiselle Lafontaine. They noticed I was nervous and not my usual self, so I finally told them what had been troubling me.

Mademoiselle laughed, but Madame Perrodon looked concerned.

"By the way," Mademoiselle said playfully, "the long path behind Carmilla's window is supposed to be haunted."

"Nonsense!" Madame Perrodon snapped. "And where did you hear that?"

"Martin told me," she replied. "He said that twice, when he came early in the morning to fix the yard gate, he saw the same woman walking down the tree-lined path."

"Well, that's not surprising," Madame said. "Plenty of people are up early to tend to the cows near the river."

"Maybe," Mademoiselle admitted, "but Martin was terrified. I've never seen someone look so scared."

"We can't mention this to Carmilla," I said quickly. "She can see that path from her window, and she's an even bigger coward than I am."

That day, Carmilla came downstairs later than usual.

"I was so scared last night," she said as soon as we were alone. "If I hadn't had that charm I bought from the little hunchback—the one I was so mean to—I think I would have seen something truly awful. I had a nightmare about something dark creeping around my bed. When I woke up, I was terrified because I thought I saw a shadowy figure near the fireplace. But the moment I reached under my pillow and touched the charm, it disappeared! If I hadn't had it, I'm sure something horrible would have appeared and strangled me, like it did to those poor people we heard about."

"Listen to this," I said, and I told her about my own terrifying night. She looked horrified.

"Did you have the charm with you?" she asked urgently.

"No," I admitted. "I had left it in the vase in the drawing room. But after hearing what you said, I'll definitely keep it with me tonight."

Even now, I can't fully understand how I managed to sleep in my room alone again that night. I remember clearly that I pinned the charm to my pillow before going to bed. I fell asleep almost immediately and, to my surprise, slept even better than usual.

The next night was the same. I had a deep, peaceful sleep, free from nightmares.

But in the morning, I woke up feeling strangely drained. I wasn't exactly sick, but I felt weak and oddly sad. Strangely, the feeling was almost pleasant in a way, like a soft, dreamy kind of sadness.

"Well, I told you so," Carmilla said when I told her about my restful sleep. "I slept wonderfully too! I pinned the charm to my nightdress this time instead of keeping it too far away. I'm sure it was all in our heads—except for the dreams. I used to think nightmares were caused by evil spirits, but our doctor told me that's not true. He said it's just an illness passing by, like a fever that knocks on the door but doesn't come inside."

"And what do you think the charm actually is?" I asked.

"It must have been soaked in some kind of medicine," she said. "It's probably meant to protect against bad air or sickness."

"So it only works on the body?"

"Of course," she said. "You don't really think evil spirits are afraid of a little ribbon or perfume, do you? No, these illnesses attack the nerves and the brain, but the charm repels them before they can take hold. That's what helped us. There's nothing magical about it—it's just science."

I wanted to believe her completely, but I couldn't shake the feeling that something else was going on. Still, I tried to push my doubts aside, and little by little, the fear started to fade.

For several nights, I slept deeply and peacefully. But every morning, I still woke up feeling exhausted. There was a strange heaviness inside me that I couldn't explain, as if something was slowly draining my energy.

More and more, I felt different—like I wasn't myself anymore. A deep sadness crept over me, but I didn't want to fight it. It wasn't a sharp, painful sadness; it was soft and almost comforting.

I began to think about death in a way I never had before. The idea didn't frighten me as much as I thought it should. Instead, it settled inside me, gentle and quiet, like a thought that had always been waiting there.

I accepted whatever was happening to me without question.

I refused to believe I was sick, and I didn't want to tell my father or have a doctor called. Meanwhile, Carmilla became even more attached to me. Her strange moments of affection grew more frequent, and the weaker I became, the more intensely she watched me. Sometimes, the way she looked at me felt almost insane, and it sent a chill through me.

Without realizing it, I had fallen into the grip of an illness unlike any other. At first, there was something strangely appealing about it that made me accept the way it drained my strength. But that feeling didn't last forever. Over time, a deep sense of horror crept in, growing stronger until it consumed my entire life.

At first, though, the changes felt pleasant. That was the dangerous part—before I even realized it, I had stepped onto a path from which I could not turn back.

Strange feelings came to me in my sleep. The most common was a pleasant, cool sensation, like swimming against the gentle current of a river. Soon, these feelings were joined by dreams—long, endless dreams that I could never fully remember. I couldn't recall the places, the people, or the events, yet they left behind a terrible sense of exhaustion, as if I had lived through something dark and dangerous.

Whenever I woke from these dreams, I had the same eerie memory: I had been in a nearly pitch-black place, speaking with people I couldn't see. And always, there was one distinct voice—a deep, distant voice of a woman that filled me with both awe and fear.

Sometimes, I felt something brushing against my face and neck, as if a hand had softly traced along my skin. Other times, I felt warm lips pressing against my throat, lingering longer each time. My heart would pound, my breath would quicken, and then a feeling of choking panic would take over. The fear built until I lost control, and my mind slipped into unconsciousness.

Three weeks had passed since this strange sickness first took hold of me.

The past week had taken a toll on my appearance. My skin had grown pale, and dark circles had formed under my eyes. My body felt weak, and I moved more slowly than before.

My father often asked if I was unwell, but I stubbornly insisted that I felt fine. In a way, I wasn't lying—I had no fever, no real pain, nothing that would suggest an ordinary illness. It felt more like something was affecting my mind rather than my body. No matter how horrible I felt, I kept it all to myself, unable to explain it even if I wanted to.

It couldn't be the same sickness that the villagers feared—the one they called the work of the oupire. Those victims never lasted more than a few days before they died, while I had already suffered for weeks.

Carmilla also mentioned having strange dreams and feeling feverish, but her symptoms weren't nearly as bad as mine. And mine were terrifying. If I had fully understood what was happening to me, I would have begged for help. But something kept me from thinking clearly, as if my mind were clouded by some unknown force.

Then, one night, I had a dream unlike the others. It led me to a discovery I could never have imagined.

Instead of the usual distant voice in the darkness, I heard something new—gentle yet terrifying:

"Your mother warns you—beware of the assassin."

At that exact moment, a light suddenly appeared, and I saw Carmilla standing at the foot of my bed. She was dressed in her white nightgown, but from her chin down to her feet, she was covered in a dark red stain—blood.

I woke up screaming.

The only thought in my mind was that Carmilla was being attacked. I jumped out of bed, and the next thing I knew, I was standing in the hallway, crying for help.

Madame Perrodon and Mademoiselle Lafontaine rushed out of their rooms, alarmed. A lamp was always left burning in the hallway, and when they saw me standing there in distress, they quickly asked what had happened.

I insisted that we check on Carmilla.

We ran to her door and knocked—but there was no answer.

We knocked again, louder. Nothing. Soon, our knocking turned into pounding. We shouted her name, but she didn't respond.

A sudden fear gripped us. The door was locked.

Panicked, we ran back to my room and rang the bell over and over, hoping to wake the servants. If my father's room had been closer, we would have called for him immediately, but he was too far away, and none of us had the courage to go alone to find him.

Finally, servants came running up the stairs. In the meantime, I had thrown on my dressing gown and slippers, as had Madame and Mademoiselle.

When we heard the voices of the servants outside, we hurried out of my room and tried calling Carmilla's name again. No answer.

I ordered the men to break down the door.

With a heavy crash, the lock gave way, and we all lifted our lamps, peering inside.

The room was exactly as I had left it when I said goodnight to Carmilla. Nothing was disturbed. Everything was in its place.

But Carmilla was gone.

Chapter VIII
Search

When we saw that the room was completely untouched—except for the way we had forced our way inside—we started to calm down. Soon, we gathered ourselves enough to send the servants away.

Mademoiselle suggested that Carmilla might have been startled awake by all the noise at her door and, in a panic, jumped out of bed and hid somewhere—maybe in a closet or behind a curtain—too afraid to come out while the servants were still there.

So, we searched again and called out for her.

Nothing.

Our confusion and worry only grew.

We checked the windows—they were locked.

I begged Carmilla, if she was hiding, to stop playing such a cruel joke and come out. Still, there was no answer.

At that point, I was convinced she wasn't in the room at all. She also wasn't in her dressing room, which was still locked from the inside. There was no way she could have passed through it.

I was completely lost.

Had Carmilla somehow found a hidden passage? The old housekeeper had once mentioned secret tunnels in the schloss, though no one remembered exactly where they were. Maybe that was the answer?

Time would tell. For now, we were left in total confusion.

Since it was past four in the morning, I decided to spend the rest of the night in Madame's room.

But when the sun rose, the mystery remained.

The whole household was in chaos. My father led the servants in searching every part of the castle and the surrounding grounds. But there was no sign of Carmilla.

People began to whisper that the stream should be searched. My father was beside himself—what would he tell the poor girl's mother when she returned?

As for me, I was in my own kind of distress, though it was different from my father's.

The morning was spent in worry.

By one o'clock, there was still no news.

I hurried up to Carmilla's room—only to find her standing at her dressing table.

I froze, unable to believe my own eyes.

She saw me and lifted a finger, motioning for me to come closer.

Her face was pale and frightened.

Overwhelmed with relief, I ran to her, wrapping her in my arms, kissing her, overcome with joy. I rushed to ring the bell, eager to bring everyone in and end my father's distress.

"Carmilla, where have you been? We've been terrified! How did you get back?" I asked breathlessly.

She gave a small, uneasy smile.

"Last night was full of strange things," she said.

"For heaven's sake, tell me what happened," I begged.

She hesitated before answering.

"I went to sleep after two o'clock," she explained. "I locked my doors as always—both the one leading to the dressing room and the one opening into the hallway. My sleep was peaceful, without dreams. But when I woke up just now, I was lying on the sofa in the dressing room. The door between the rooms was open, and the door leading to the hall had been forced."

Her voice wavered.

"How could all of that have happened without waking me? I wake so easily. Even the slightest noise can startle me awake—so how could I be taken from my bed without noticing? It makes no sense."

By then, Madame, Mademoiselle, my father, and several servants had arrived.

Carmilla was bombarded with questions and relieved welcomes, though she had no answers. She seemed the most confused of us all, unable to explain anything.

My father paced the room, deep in thought.

I noticed Carmilla watching him carefully for a moment, her expression unreadable.

Once the servants left and Mademoiselle had gone to fetch some valerian drops to help calm Carmilla, my father finally spoke.

He walked over to Carmilla, took her hand gently, and led her to the sofa.

Sitting beside her, he asked, "Would you be upset if I make a guess and ask you a question?"

Carmilla gave a tired smile.

"You have every right to ask whatever you want," she said. "I'll tell you anything I can. But my story is just confusion and darkness—I know absolutely nothing. You may ask, but of course, you know there are things my mother has forbidden me to speak about."

"Of course," my father said kindly. "I won't ask about those matters. But here is what I find so astonishing—how were you moved from your locked room without waking up? Both doors were secured from the inside, and the windows were untouched. It should have been impossible.

"So, here is my question," he continued, watching her closely.

"Have you ever been known to walk in your sleep?"

"I haven't since I was very young," Carmilla said.

"But you did sleepwalk when you were little?" my father asked.

"Yes, I've been told so many times by my old nurse."

My father smiled and nodded.

"Well, then, here's what must have happened," he said. "You got up in your sleep, unlocked the door—but instead of leaving the key in the lock like you usually do, you took it out, locked the door from the outside, and then carried the key with you. You probably wandered into one of the many rooms on this floor—or maybe even upstairs or downstairs. There are so many rooms, closets, and pieces of heavy furniture in this old house, it would take a whole week to search it all. Do you see what I mean?"

"I understand... but not everything," Carmilla replied.

"And how do you explain her waking up on the sofa in the dressing room, Papa? We searched that room so carefully before," I asked.

"She must have gone in there after your search—still asleep—and only woke up naturally after that," he said. "She was probably just as surprised as we were to find herself there."

Then, with a laugh, he added, "I only wish all mysteries could be explained as simply and harmlessly as yours, Carmilla. No need to worry about being drugged, no locks being tampered with, no burglars, no poisoners, no witches—nothing to make you or anyone else afraid."

Carmilla looked as lovely as ever, her delicate features even more striking with that soft, dreamy look that always made her seem unique.

I noticed my father glancing between us, and after a moment, he sighed.

"I just wish my poor Laura looked more like herself," he said.

With that, our fears were put to rest, and Carmilla was back with her friends.

Chapter IX
The Doctor

Since Carmilla refused to let anyone stay in her room at night, my father arranged for a servant to sleep outside her door. That way, if she tried to leave again, she could be stopped before she got far.

That night passed without any trouble. The next morning, a doctor arrived unexpectedly—my father had called for him without telling me.

Madame Perrodon took me to the library, where the doctor, a serious-looking man with white hair and glasses, was waiting.

I told him everything, and as I spoke, his face became more and more serious. We stood near one of the large windows, facing each other, and by the time I finished, he was leaning against the wall, staring at me with concern—and maybe even a little fear.

After thinking for a moment, he asked Madame if he could speak to my father.

A servant was sent to fetch him, and when my father entered the room, he smiled and said, "Doctor, I suppose you're going to tell me I'm a fool for bringing you here. I hope I am."

But when he saw the doctor's grim expression, his smile quickly faded.

The two of them spoke in hushed voices near the window, deep in discussion. The room was large, and Madame and I stood at the far end, burning with curiosity, but unable to hear a single word. The thick walls and the window's deep recess made their voices barely audible, and we could only see my father's arm and part of his shoulder as he leaned in to listen.

After a while, my father turned to face the room. His face looked pale and troubled, and I thought I saw worry in his eyes.

"Laura, dear, come here for a moment," he said. Then he turned to Madame. "We won't need to trouble you just yet, according to the doctor."

I walked over, starting to feel uneasy. I had been feeling weak, but not exactly sick, and I always thought strength was something that could come back whenever you wanted.

My father took my hand but kept looking at the doctor. "This is very strange. I don't quite understand it. Laura, pay close attention to Dr. Spielsberg and try to remember clearly."

The doctor asked, "You said that on the night of your first strange dream, you felt something like two needles pricking your skin. It was near your neck, correct? Does it still feel sore?"

"No, not at all," I answered.

"Can you show me exactly where you think it happened?"

I pointed just below my throat. My dress covered the area, but I knew where the sensation had been.

"Now you can see for yourself," the doctor said. "Laura, do you mind if your father lowers your collar just a little? I need to check for signs of the illness you've been experiencing."

I agreed, since it was only a small adjustment.

My father leaned in to look, then suddenly exclaimed, "Good heavens—it's really there!" His face turned pale.

"You see it now with your own eyes," the doctor said grimly, as if confirming his suspicion.

"What is it?" I asked, feeling a wave of fear.

"Nothing serious, my dear," the doctor reassured me. "Just a small blue mark, about the size of the tip of your little finger." Then, turning back to my father, he added, "Now, the question is—what should we do next?"

"Is it dangerous?" I asked anxiously.

"I don't think so," the doctor replied. "There's no reason why you shouldn't start getting better soon. That's the spot where you first felt the strangling sensation, correct?"

"Yes," I said.

"And when you described that cold feeling, like a stream of water moving against you—did it also seem to come from that spot?"

"I think so," I said hesitantly. "Yes, it probably did."

The doctor gave my father a knowing look. "You see?" he said. "Shall I speak to Madame?"

"Yes, of course," my father agreed.

The doctor called Madame over and said, "Miss Laura is not well, though I don't believe it's anything too serious. However, we do need to take certain precautions. For now, the most important thing is that she is never left alone—not for a single moment. That is absolutely necessary."

"We can count on your kindness, Madame, I'm sure," my father added.

Madame quickly reassured him.

"And you, dear Laura, I know you'll follow the doctor's instructions," he continued.

Then, turning back to the doctor, he said, "I'd like to ask your opinion about another young lady who has similar symptoms to Laura's, though much milder. She's our guest. But since you mentioned you'll be passing by again this evening, why don't you stay for supper? You can see her then. She usually doesn't come downstairs until the afternoon."

"Thank you," the doctor said. "I'll be here around seven this evening."

After reminding us of his instructions, he left with my father. I watched them walk back and forth outside, deep in serious conversation near the moat in front of the castle. The doctor never returned inside. Instead, I saw him mount his horse, say his goodbyes, and ride away toward the east, disappearing into the forest.

Almost at the same time, a messenger arrived from Dranfield with the day's letters. He handed the mailbag to my father, who looked through it.

Meanwhile, Madame and I tried to figure out why the doctor and my father had insisted so strongly on their instructions. Later, Madame told me she suspected the doctor was worried about a sudden attack—maybe some kind of seizure—that could be dangerous or even fatal if help wasn't nearby.

That thought never crossed my mind. Instead, I assumed the rule was just to make sure I didn't overexert myself or do anything reckless, like eating too much fruit or running around too much—things young people are often warned about.

About half an hour later, my father came inside holding a letter.

"This was delayed," he said. "It's from General Spielsdorf. He could have arrived yesterday, or maybe he won't come until tomorrow. Or he might even be on his way now."

He handed me the open letter, but he didn't seem happy about it. Usually, when guests were coming—especially someone he cared for as much as the General—he would be pleased. But now, he looked almost as if he wished the General would turn back and never come. There was clearly something on his mind that he wasn't ready to share.

"Papa," I said suddenly, touching his arm and looking up at him. "Will you tell me the truth?"

"Maybe," he said, gently smoothing my hair over my forehead.

"Does the doctor think I'm very sick?"

"No, dear," he replied. "He believes that if we take the right steps, you'll recover soon. In a day or two, you should be much better." His tone was calm, but something about it seemed a little dry and distant. Then he added, "I just wish the General had chosen another time to visit. I would have preferred for you to be completely well when he arrived."

"But please, Papa, tell me—what does the doctor think is wrong with me?"

"Nothing," he said quickly. "Don't ask so many questions." His voice was sharper than usual, and I was so surprised that I must have looked hurt. He sighed, kissed me on the forehead, and added, "You'll know everything in a day or two. That's all I can say for now. But don't worry yourself over it."

Then he turned and left the room.

I was still sitting there, trying to make sense of his odd behavior, when he came back just a moment later.

"I almost forgot," he said. "I'm going to Karnstein today, and the carriage will be ready at noon. You and Madame will come with me. I need to meet with the priest who lives near the ruins. Since Carmilla hasn't seen the place yet, she can follow later with Mademoiselle. They'll bring supplies for a picnic in the old castle."

At noon, I was ready, and soon after, my father, Madame, and I set off on our drive.

Once we crossed the drawbridge, we turned right and followed the road over the steep Gothic bridge, heading west toward the abandoned village and the ruined castle of Karnstein.

The journey was beautiful. The landscape was full of gentle hills and dips, all covered with trees that looked wild and untouched. Nothing about the forest felt planned or trimmed like a formal garden—it was nature as it had always been.

The road twisted and turned, following the shape of the hills and valleys. Sometimes it curved unexpectedly, winding around steep slopes and dipping into shadowy hollows, giving us new and breathtaking views at every turn.

At one of these turns, we suddenly came across General Spielsdorf. He was riding toward us, followed by a servant on horseback. Behind them, a small cart carried his luggage.

As soon as our carriage stopped, the General dismounted. After the usual greetings, we convinced him to ride with us instead of continuing on horseback. He sent his horse ahead with his servant to the schloss, and we made room for him in the carriage.

Chapter X
Bereaved

It had been about ten months since we had last seen the General, but in that short time, he had aged many years. He looked thinner, and the warm, calm expression he once had was replaced by a shadow of worry and anger. His deep blue eyes, always sharp, now held a harder, more intense look beneath his thick gray eyebrows. It wasn't just grief that had changed him—there was something more, a deeper rage that had taken hold of him.

We hadn't been driving for long before he started speaking, in his usual straightforward way, about the terrible loss of his beloved niece and ward. His voice was filled with bitterness and fury as he cursed the "evil forces" that had taken her from him. He was so angry that he even questioned how Heaven could allow such dark and wicked things to happen.

My father, sensing that something unusual had occurred, asked if he would share the details, as long as it wouldn't be too painful for him to talk about.

"I would tell you everything," the General replied, "but you wouldn't believe me."

"Why not?" my father asked.

"Because you only believe in things that fit with your own ideas and beliefs," the General said sharply. "I used to be the same way, but I've learned better."

"Try me," my father said. "I'm not as stubborn as you think. Besides, I know you always need proof before you believe anything, so I trust your judgment."

"You're right about that," the General said. "I don't believe in strange or supernatural things without good reason. But what I've been through is beyond belief. I've been tricked by a force that isn't human."

Even though my father had just said he trusted the General's reasoning, I saw a brief look of doubt in his eyes. For a moment, he seemed to wonder if the General had lost his sanity.

Luckily, the General didn't notice. He was too busy staring into the trees along the road, his expression dark and thoughtful.

"You're going to the Karnstein ruins?" he suddenly asked.

"Yes, it just so happens that we are," my father replied. "Why? Were you planning to visit them as well?"

"Yes," the General said. "That's why I wanted to ask if you could take me there. I have something important to do. There's an old chapel there, isn't there? With the tombs of that long-extinct family?"

"There is," my father said. "It's a fascinating place. What, are you planning to claim the title and estate for yourself?" he joked.

My father's lighthearted remark didn't get so much as a smile from the General. Instead, his expression grew even grimmer.

"No," he said gruffly. "I intend to dig some of those old Karnsteins out of their graves. And with God's help, I plan to rid the earth of monsters so that decent people can sleep safely in their beds. I have strange things to tell you, things that I would have laughed at just a few months ago."

My father looked at him again, but this time with real concern, not doubt. His eyes sharpened with curiosity and alarm.

"The Karnstein family has been gone for over a hundred years," my father said. "My late wife was distantly related to them on her mother's side. But the family name and title have long disappeared. Their castle is in ruins. Even the village is abandoned. No one has lived there for fifty years."

"That's true," the General said, nodding. "I've learned a great deal about them since I last saw you. Things that will shock you. But I should tell you everything in the order it happened."

"You saw my dear ward," he continued, his voice softer now. "She was like a daughter to me. No one could have been more beautiful, and just three months ago, she was full of life."

"Yes," my father agreed, his face clouding with sympathy. "When I last saw her, she was absolutely lovely. I was so saddened to hear of her passing, my friend. I can only imagine how painful this loss is for you."

The two men clasped hands in a quiet moment of shared sorrow. The old soldier's eyes filled with tears, and he didn't try to hide them.

"We have been friends for many years," the General said. "I knew you would understand my grief. I have no children of my own, and she brought so much love and joy into my home. But all of that is gone now. My remaining years may not be many, but before I die, I hope to bring justice to the creatures that stole my child. I hope to serve Heaven's vengeance upon them!"

"You said you would tell the story from the beginning," my father said. "Please do. I assure you, it is not just curiosity that makes me ask."

By this time, we had reached the spot where the road from Drunstall—the one the General had traveled—split from the road we were taking to Karnstein.

"How far are the ruins from here?" the General asked, glancing ahead impatiently.

"About half a league," my father replied.

"Good," the General said. "Then I have just enough time to tell you everything."

Chapter XI
The Story

"Of course," said the General, taking a deep breath before starting one of the strangest stories I had ever heard.

"My dear child was so excited about the visit you had planned with your lovely daughter." He paused and gave me a polite bow, though there was sadness in his expression. "Before that, we had accepted an invitation from my old friend Count Carlsfeld, who lives in a castle about six leagues beyond Karnstein. He was hosting grand celebrations in honor of the Grand Duke Charles, and we were invited to attend."

"Yes, I heard they were quite spectacular," my father said.

"They were beyond magnificent! The Count's generosity knows no limits. The night that changed everything was during a masquerade ball. The gardens were open, the trees were strung with colorful lanterns, and fireworks filled the sky—more dazzling than anything I had seen, even in Paris. And the music! Music is my greatest weakness, and I have never heard anything so enchanting. The finest orchestra in the world played, joined by the most talented opera singers from across Europe. As you wandered through the glowing gardens, with the moon shining over the grand château, you would suddenly hear angelic voices drifting from the trees or echoing across the lake from boats. It felt like stepping into a dream, like I had been transported back to the poetry and magic of my youth.

"When the fireworks ended and the ballroom opened, we returned inside to the beautifully decorated halls filled with dancers. A masked ball is always a magical sight, but I had never seen anything so breathtaking before.

"It was a gathering of nobility, and I was probably the only ordinary person there.

"My dear girl was absolutely glowing that night. She chose not to wear a mask, and the joy and excitement on her face made her even more beautiful. I noticed a young woman, dressed elegantly and wearing a mask, who seemed to be watching my ward with great interest. I had noticed her earlier in the evening, standing in the grand hall and again on the terrace beneath the castle windows, always observing my child. She was accompanied by an older woman, also masked, dressed in a dignified and refined style that suggested she was someone of high status.

"If the young woman had not been wearing a mask, I might not have thought much of it. But now I am sure—she was watching my ward.

"We were in one of the large reception rooms when my dear child, after dancing, sat down to rest in a chair near the door. I stood close by. The two women approached, and the younger one sat beside my ward while the elder remained standing next to me, speaking in a quiet voice to her companion.

"Then, taking advantage of the anonymity of the mask, the older woman turned to me and spoke as if we were old friends, calling me by name. She recalled places where we had supposedly met—at court, at grand gatherings. She mentioned small details from my past, things I had long forgotten but that, as soon as she spoke of them, came rushing back into my memory.

"I became increasingly curious to know who she was. Every time I tried to figure it out, she cleverly avoided my questions, enjoying my confusion. Her knowledge of my life was baffling, and she seemed to take pleasure in keeping me guessing, watching as I struggled to piece things together.

"Meanwhile, the young lady, whom the older woman called Millarca, had struck up a conversation with my ward just as easily. She introduced herself by saying that her mother was an old acquaintance of mine. She spoke freely, taking advantage of the secrecy of the masks. She complimented my child's dress, admired her beauty, and made witty observations about the people in the ballroom. My ward laughed at her remarks, and the two of them quickly became comfortable with one another. After a while, the young stranger lowered her mask, revealing an incredibly beautiful face. Neither my ward nor I had ever seen her before, but there was something so enchanting about her that it was impossible not to be drawn in. My poor girl was completely taken with her. I had never seen such an instant bond between two people— except, perhaps, for the stranger herself, who seemed equally captivated.

"While they talked, I continued trying to uncover the older woman's identity.

"'You've completely confused me,' I said, laughing. 'Isn't that enough? Won't you be kind and take off your mask so we can be on even ground?'

"'What an unreasonable request,' she replied playfully. 'You want me to give up my advantage? Besides, how do you know you would even recognize me? Time changes people.'

"'As you can see,' I said with a small, likely sad, smile.

"'As wise men always say,' she added. 'And how can you be sure that seeing my face would help you?'

"'I'm willing to take that risk,' I answered. 'You can't pretend to be an old woman—your figure gives you away.'

"'And yet, many years have passed since you last saw me—or rather, since you saw me and I saw you,' she corrected herself. 'That girl over there, Millarca, is my daughter. So, I cannot be young anymore, even in the eyes of someone as generous as you. And perhaps I do not wish to be compared to the way you remember me.'

"'You have no mask to remove,' she continued. 'You offer me nothing in return.'

"'Then I ask only for your kindness in revealing yourself,' I said.

"'And I ask for yours in letting me keep my mask on,' she replied with a smile."

"Well then, will you at least tell me whether you are French or German? You speak both languages so perfectly."

"I don't think I'll tell you that, General," she replied. "You're planning a surprise and choosing just the right approach."

"At the very least, you won't deny this," I said. "Since you've allowed me the honor of speaking with you, I should know how to address you properly. Should I call you Madame la Comtesse?"

She laughed, and I could tell she was about to dodge my question again—if, that is, anything in this conversation had really been left to chance. Looking back, I now believe every detail of this meeting had been carefully planned with great skill.

"As for that—" she began, but before she could finish, a man dressed in black suddenly appeared. He was elegantly dressed, with an air of distinction, but his face was the palest I had ever seen—so pale it almost looked lifeless. He was not in costume, just wearing the formal evening attire of a gentleman. Without smiling, but with a deep and respectful bow, he said:

"Would Madame la Comtesse allow me to speak for a moment? I have something to say that may interest her."

The lady turned to him quickly and placed a finger to her lips, signaling for silence. Then she turned back to me and said, "Save my seat, General. I'll be back after a quick word."

With that, she stepped aside with the man in black, speaking with him in hushed but serious tones. After a few minutes, they slowly walked away together into the crowd, and I lost sight of them.

I spent the next few minutes trying to guess who this mysterious woman might be. She seemed to know me well, and I was determined to figure out her name, title, and where she was from before she returned. Just as I was about to turn and join the conversation between my ward and the Countess's daughter, she came back, still accompanied by the pale man in black.

"I will return shortly to inform Madame la Comtesse when her carriage is ready," he said, bowing before walking away.

Chapter XII
A Petition

"Then we must say goodbye to Madame la Comtesse, but I hope it will only be for a little while," I said with a polite bow.

"It could be just a few hours, or it might be several weeks," she replied. "It was bad timing that he spoke to me just now." She paused before asking, "Do you recognize me yet?"

I assured her that I did not.

"You will," she said, "but not yet. We have known each other much longer than you might guess. I cannot reveal my identity just now, but in three weeks, I will pass by your beautiful home. I have been asking about it. I plan to stop by for a short visit and renew a friendship that brings back so many happy memories.

"But just now, I have received news like a thunderbolt. I must leave immediately and travel nearly a hundred miles in a complicated route as quickly as I can. My troubles are piling up. I would ask you for something unusual, but because I must keep my identity secret, I hesitate.

"My poor daughter has not fully recovered from an accident. Her horse fell while she was watching a hunt, and her nerves are still shaken. The doctor has warned that she must not exert herself for some time. That is why we have been traveling slowly, no more than six leagues a day. But now, I must travel day and night on an urgent mission of life and death. When we meet again, I will be able to explain everything, and there will be no need for secrecy."

She then made her request, but in a way that seemed like she was offering me a favor rather than asking for one. It was in her tone—though I believe she was unaware of it. Still, her words were humble and respectful. She simply asked if I would take care of her daughter while she was away.

Given the situation, it was a bold and unusual request. However, she disarmed me by addressing every possible objection herself and placing all her trust in my honor. At that moment, as if fate had arranged it, my dear child came to my side and quietly begged me to invite Millarca to stay with us. She had just been talking to her and was sure that, if her mother allowed it, Millarca would love to visit.

At another time, I would have told her to wait until we at least knew more about them. But I had no time to think. Both the Countess and my daughter urged me at once. And I must admit, the young lady's beauty and graceful manner, along with her noble presence, influenced me. Overwhelmed, I gave in and agreed to take care of the girl her mother called Millarca.

The Countess gestured for her daughter to come closer. Millarca listened seriously as her mother explained, in general terms, that she had to leave suddenly on urgent business. She also told her that she would be staying in my care, adding that I was one of her oldest and dearest friends.

Of course, I said all the polite things that the situation required. But as I thought about it, I realized I was now in a position I wasn't entirely comfortable with.

Just then, the pale man in black returned. With perfect manners, he escorted the Countess from the room.

Something about the way this man behaved made me feel that the Countess was far more important than her simple title suggested.

As she was leaving, she gave me one last instruction: no one was to try to find out more about her than what I might have already guessed. Our host, who had invited her, understood her reasons.

"But here," she added, "neither my daughter nor I can safely stay for more than a day. I made the mistake of removing my mask for just a moment about an hour ago, and too late, I thought you had seen me. So I decided to speak with you. If I had known for certain that you recognized me, I would have trusted in your honor to keep my secret for a few weeks. But now, I am sure you did not see me clearly. Still, if you suspect, or later begin to suspect who I am, I trust you to keep it to yourself. My daughter will also keep the secret, and I know you will remind her from time to time, just in case she forgets and accidentally reveals it."

She whispered a few words to Millarca, kissed her quickly twice, then hurried away with the pale gentleman in black. A moment later, they disappeared into the crowd.

"In the next room," said Millarca, "there is a window that looks out onto the front entrance. I'd like to see my mother leave and wave goodbye to her."

Of course, we agreed and walked with her to the window.

Outside, we saw a grand, old-fashioned carriage surrounded by couriers and footmen. The pale man in black carefully wrapped a heavy velvet cloak around the Countess's shoulders and pulled the hood over her head. She gave him a small nod and lightly touched his hand. He bowed deeply several times as the carriage door closed, and then it rolled away.

"She's gone," Millarca sighed.

"She's gone," I echoed, finally realizing how careless I had been to agree so quickly without thinking it through.

"She didn't even look up," the young girl said sadly.

"Maybe the Countess had taken off her mask and didn't want to show her face," I suggested. "Or she might not have known you were watching from the window."

She sighed and looked at me. She was so beautiful that my doubts faded. I regretted even briefly questioning my decision to welcome her, and I resolved to make it up to her for my unspoken hesitation.

The young lady put her mask back on and joined my ward in convincing me to return to the gardens, where the concert was about to start again. We did, strolling along the terrace beneath the castle windows. Millarca quickly became comfortable with us, entertaining us with lively stories about the important people around us. Her tales, though never mean-spirited, were full of wit, and I, having been away from high society for some time, found them fascinating. I thought about how much fun she would bring to our quiet evenings at home.

The ball lasted until the sun was almost rising. Since the Grand Duke wished to dance until morning, no one could leave before him.

As we made our way through a crowded ballroom, my ward suddenly asked where Millarca had gone. I thought she had been beside her, while she believed Millarca had been with me. But in truth, we had lost her.

No matter how hard I searched, I couldn't find her. I feared she had gotten separated from us in the crowd, mistaken other guests for us, and then wandered off in the vast gardens.

Now, more than ever, I realized how foolish I had been to take responsibility for a young lady whose full name I didn't even know. Worse still, I had promised not to reveal anything about her mother, which made asking about her nearly impossible.

Morning came, and by daylight, I had given up looking for her. It wasn't until almost two o'clock in the afternoon that we finally heard news of her.

A servant knocked on my niece's door, saying that a young lady, visibly upset, had asked him desperately where she could find General Baron Spielsdorf and his daughter, in whose care she had been left.

Despite the small mistake in her wording, it was clear that our missing guest had returned. If only we had never found her!

She told my poor child a story to explain her absence. She said that, after searching everywhere for us, she had ended up in the housekeeper's bedroom in despair and had fallen into a deep sleep. The exhaustion from the long night had been too much, and she had only just woken up.

That same day, Millarca came home with us. Despite everything, I was relieved to have found such a charming companion for my dear girl.

Chapter XIII
The Woodman

There were soon some troubling signs. Millarca often complained of feeling weak and tired, blaming it on her recent illness. She rarely left her room before late afternoon. More strangely, although she always locked her door from the inside and didn't open it until the maid came to help her dress, it became clear that she sometimes left her room at night or early in the morning. People saw her from the castle windows at dawn, walking through the trees as if in a trance, always heading east.

I started to believe she was sleepwalking, but that didn't explain everything. How did she get out of her locked room? How did she leave the house without opening a door or a window?

As I puzzled over these strange events, a more urgent fear took hold of me—my beloved child's health was failing. Her decline was mysterious and terrifying.

First, she had terrible nightmares. Then she started seeing strange figures—sometimes a shadowy beast, sometimes a figure that looked like Millarca—pacing at the foot of her bed. Then came the strange sensations. At first, she described it as an icy stream flowing over her chest, which wasn't painful but felt unnatural. Later, she felt sharp stabs, like two long needles piercing her throat. Soon after, she started experiencing a choking sensation, as if something was strangling her in her sleep, until she would finally pass out.

I listened closely to every word the kind old General said, because by this time, our carriage had reached a quiet grassy path leading to a deserted village. No smoke had risen from its chimneys for over fifty years.

Hearing him describe the exact same symptoms I had been suffering made me shudder. This was the girl who was supposed to visit our home, the one who had died under mysterious circumstances. But what shook me even more was hearing him describe strange habits that perfectly matched those of our beautiful guest, Carmilla.

As we rode through a clearing in the forest, I suddenly found myself looking up at the ruins of the abandoned village, with the crumbling towers of an old castle rising beyond it. Tall trees surrounded the remains of the once-great fortress. I felt like I was in a dream as I stepped out of the carriage. No one spoke; we all had too much to think about.

We climbed the hill and walked through the vast, empty halls, winding staircases, and dark corridors of the ruined castle.

"So this was once the grand home of the Karnsteins," the old General finally said as he stood by a large window, looking out at the dense forest stretching beyond the village. "They were a cursed family, and their bloody history was written here. It is unfair that even in death, they continue to haunt and harm the living." He pointed to a crumbling stone chapel, partly hidden by trees at the bottom of the hill. "That is the Karnstein family chapel," he said.

Then he paused, listening. "I hear the sound of an axe," he added. "A woodcutter must be working nearby. He might know where to find the grave of Mircalla, Countess of Karnstein. Peasants often remember the history of noble families long after the aristocrats themselves have forgotten it."

"We have a portrait of Mircalla at home," my father said. "Would you like to see it?"

"There will be time for that later," the General replied. "I believe I have already seen her in person. One reason I came here earlier than planned was to search this very chapel."

"You've seen the Countess Mircalla?" my father asked in shock. "She's been dead for over a hundred years!"

"Not as dead as you think," the General replied darkly.

My father looked at him in confusion, and for a moment, I thought I saw suspicion in his eyes again. But despite the General's obvious anger and hatred, there was no madness in his words.

As we stepped under the heavy stone arch of the ancient chapel—large enough to be considered a small church—the General's voice grew serious. "I have only one purpose left in my life, and that is to bring justice to the creature who stole my child. I thank God that it is still possible for a mortal man to take revenge."

"What revenge are you talking about?" my father asked, looking more bewildered by the second.

"I mean to cut off the creature's head," the General said, his face red with fury. He stomped his foot, the sound echoing through the empty ruins, and raised his clenched fist as if gripping an invisible axe, shaking it violently in the air.

"What?" my father exclaimed, looking more confused than ever.

"To behead her," the General repeated.

"Cut off her head?"

"Yes! With a hatchet, a spade—anything that will slice through her cursed throat. You'll understand soon," he said, his voice trembling with anger. Then, moving quickly ahead, he gestured toward a wooden beam lying on the overgrown chapel floor. "That will do for a seat. Your poor child must be exhausted—let her rest while I finish my terrible story."

I was relieved to sit down, and while I did, the General called over a woodcutter who had been clearing branches that leaned against the old chapel walls. The man, holding his axe, stepped forward to speak with us.

Unfortunately, he didn't know anything about the old gravestones, but he told us about an elderly forest ranger who was staying at the priest's house two miles away. This old man, he said, knew every grave belonging to the Karnstein family. He offered to fetch him, saying he could be back in about half an hour if we lent him a horse.

"Have you worked in this forest for long?" my father asked.

"I've been a woodcutter here all my life, sir," the man answered in his thick country accent. "So was my father before me, and his father before him, as far back as I can count. I could even show you the house in this village where my family lived."

"Why was the village abandoned?" the General asked.

"It was cursed by the dead, sir," the woodcutter explained. "Many people were attacked by revenants—spirits that returned from their graves. Some of them were tracked down, dug up, and tested in the usual ways. Once they were proven to be vampires, they were destroyed—decapitated, staked, and burned. But not before they had killed many of the villagers."

He paused, then continued, "Even after those measures, the trouble didn't end. Then, a nobleman from Moravia happened to pass through and heard about what was happening. He knew a lot about these kinds of things—many people in his country do—and he offered to rid the village of its tormentor.

"That night, when the moon was bright, he climbed the tower of this chapel, from where he could clearly see the graveyard. You can see it from that window over there. He waited and watched until he saw the vampire rise from its grave. It removed the linen burial cloths it had been wrapped in and left them beside the grave before gliding toward the village to attack the people.

"Once the nobleman saw this, he climbed down the tower, took the vampire's burial cloths, and carried them back up to the top of the steeple. When the vampire returned from its hunt and couldn't find the cloths, it flew into a rage. Then it looked up and saw the nobleman at the top of the tower. The nobleman waved the cloths at him and invited him to climb up and retrieve them.

"The vampire, desperate, accepted the challenge and started climbing the tower. But as soon as it reached the top, the nobleman drew his sword and, with a single stroke, split its skull in two. The creature tumbled down into the graveyard, and the nobleman followed it down the spiral staircase. Once he reached the ground, he cut off the vampire's head and delivered both head and body to the villagers the next day. They impaled and burned the remains, as was the custom.

"This nobleman had also been given permission by the head of the Karnstein family to remove the tomb of Mircalla, Countess of Karnstein. He did so thoroughly, and over time, people forgot exactly where her grave had been."

"Can you show us where it was?" the General asked eagerly.

The woodcutter shook his head and smiled. "No one alive could tell you that now," he said. "Some say her body was taken away, but no one knows for sure."

With that, realizing time was short, he set down his axe and hurried off to find the old ranger, leaving us to hear the rest of the General's chilling story.

Chapter XIV
The Meeting

"My beloved child," the General continued, "was getting worse by the day. The doctor treating her had no success in stopping her illness—if that's what it was. Seeing my fear, he suggested calling in another doctor for a second opinion. I sent for a well-respected physician from Gratz.

"It took several days for him to arrive. He was not only knowledgeable but also a deeply religious man. After examining my poor ward, the two doctors met in my library to discuss their findings. I waited in the next room, expecting to be called in. But instead, I heard their voices rising in an argument. It became so heated that I knocked and entered.

"I found the doctor from Gratz standing firm on his opinion while the other doctor was laughing and ridiculing him. When I walked in, they quickly fell silent.

"'Sir,' my first doctor said, 'it seems my learned colleague believes you need a magician rather than a physician.'

"The doctor from Gratz looked displeased. 'I will share my thoughts at another time in my own way,' he said. 'But, Monsieur le General, I regret to say that my skills are of no use here. However, before I leave, I have something important to suggest to you.'

"He seemed deep in thought as he sat down to write a note. I was filled with disappointment and prepared to leave, but as I turned, the first doctor shrugged and tapped his forehead as if to suggest his colleague was crazy.

"I was left with no answers. Frustrated and worried, I wandered outside. Within ten or fifteen minutes, the doctor from Gratz caught up to me. He apologized for following me but said he couldn't leave without telling me something more.

"He told me he was absolutely certain—this was no ordinary illness. No natural disease caused these symptoms. He warned me that death was very close. My ward had maybe a day, perhaps two, left to live. If we could stop the attacks in time, with great care, she might recover. But if there was just one more, it would likely kill her.

"'What kind of attack are you talking about?' I begged him to explain.

"'I've written everything down in this note,' he said, handing me the letter. 'But I must insist you do not open it unless you have a priest with you. If you read it alone, you will not believe it. It is a matter of life and death. If you cannot find a priest, only then should you read it by yourself.'

"Before leaving, he asked if I would like to meet a man who was an expert on this subject—one who might help me understand after reading the letter. He strongly urged me to invite this man to my home. Then he left.

"The priest was away, so I read the letter alone. Under any other circumstances, I would have laughed at it. But when someone you love is dying, you are willing to try anything, no matter how strange it seems.

"The letter claimed that my ward was not suffering from an illness at all but was being attacked by a vampire. The doctor insisted that the small punctures on her neck were bite marks—made by the long, thin, sharp teeth of a vampire. He described a dark bruise left by the creature's lips, which matched exactly what we had seen. Every symptom, he said, matched those of others who had been visited by such creatures.

"I did not believe in vampires, but I was so desperate that I followed the instructions anyway.

"I hid in the dark dressing room attached to my ward's bedroom, where a candle was burning. I waited silently until she was deeply asleep. As instructed in the letter, I stood by the door, peering through a small opening. My sword was on the table beside me.

"A little after one o'clock, I saw a dark shape crawl over the foot of the bed. It was hard to make out, but it looked like a shadow stretching across her bed, creeping toward her throat. Then, in an instant, it grew into a large, pulsing mass.

"For a few moments, I was frozen in shock. Then I lunged forward with my sword. The black shape shrank back, sliding down to the foot of the bed. I saw it take form—standing on the floor, glaring at me with eyes full of both fear and fury—was Millarca.

"I swung my sword at her, but before my blade could reach her, she was suddenly standing near the door, unharmed. I was horrified. I rushed at her again, striking once more, but she was gone. My sword shattered against the door.

"I cannot fully describe the chaos of that night. The whole house was awake, alarmed by the commotion. But the ghostly figure of Millarca had vanished.

"Her victim, however, was fading fast. Before the morning came, my ward had passed away."

The General was visibly shaken. None of us spoke. My father wandered a short distance away, reading the inscriptions on the crumbling tombstones. As he walked, he disappeared into a side chapel to continue his search.

The General leaned against the wall, wiping his eyes with a deep sigh.

I felt a sense of relief when I heard the voices of Carmilla and Madame approaching. But then, as their voices faded away and they did not enter, a terrible feeling crept over me.

Standing there, surrounded by ancient tombs and the ruins of a cursed family, having just listened to this horrifying tale, I was overcome with dread. The towering trees loomed above us, casting deep shadows over the silent graveyard. A shiver ran down my spine as I realized that my friends were not coming to break this eerie stillness. I was alone in the heart of this haunted place.

The old General stared at the ground, leaning on the base of a broken monument.

Through a narrow, arched doorway, decorated with a grotesque, demonic carving in the old Gothic style, I saw Carmilla step into the dimly lit chapel. Her face was as beautiful as ever.

I smiled and started to stand up, ready to greet her, but before I could speak, the General suddenly let out a cry. He grabbed the woodman's axe and rushed toward her.

As soon as she saw him, her expression twisted into something inhuman and terrifying. It happened in an instant—her face transformed with a look of pure rage, and she stepped backward like an animal about to strike. Before I could even scream, the General swung the axe at her with all his strength.

But she was too fast. She ducked under the blow, untouched, and grabbed his wrist with her small, delicate-looking hands. He tried to pull free, but his fingers lost their grip, and the axe dropped to the ground. In that same moment, Carmilla vanished.

The General staggered back against the wall, his face pale and covered in sweat. His grey hair stood on end, and he looked as if he might collapse.

It had all happened so fast. The next thing I knew, Madame was standing in front of me, her voice sharp with urgency as she repeated over and over, "Where is Mademoiselle Carmilla?"

Still shaken, I finally answered, "I don't know. I can't say. She was just here," I pointed toward the doorway where Madame had come in, "only a minute or two ago."

Madame frowned. "But I've been standing in the passageway this whole time since Mademoiselle Carmilla entered. She never came back out."

She immediately began calling for Carmilla, shouting her name down every hallway and from the windows. But there was no reply.

The General, still breathing heavily, turned to me. "She called herself Carmilla?"

"Yes," I answered.

He shook his head grimly. "That is Millarca. That is the same one who, long ago, was known as Mircalla, Countess Karnstein."

He turned to me with a look of deep concern. "Leave this cursed place at once, my poor child. Go straight to the clergyman's house and stay there until we come for you. Go now! And pray you never see Carmilla again—you will not find her here."

Chapter XV
Ordeal and Execution

As the General spoke, one of the strangest-looking men I had ever seen entered the chapel through the same door Carmilla had used.

He was tall but hunched over, with narrow shoulders and a thin frame. His face was dark and deeply wrinkled, and he wore an oddly shaped hat with a wide brim. Long, graying hair fell over his shoulders, and he had a pair of gold-rimmed spectacles perched on his nose. His movements were strange—his steps were uneven, and he swung his long arms back and forth, his gloved hands making odd gestures as if lost in thought. Though he seemed deep in concentration, he wore a constant, eerie smile.

"The very man!" the General exclaimed, clearly thrilled. "My dear Baron, what a stroke of luck to find you here! I never expected to see you so soon."

He quickly called my father over, who had just returned, and introduced him to the unusual old man, whom he addressed as the Baron. The two immediately fell into deep conversation.

The Baron pulled a rolled-up paper from his pocket and spread it over an old, crumbling tomb. He held a pencil in one hand and traced invisible lines across the paper while glancing between it and various parts of the chapel. From their intense focus, I guessed the paper must have been a map or layout of the building. As they talked, he occasionally read from a small, worn-out book with pages covered in tightly written notes.

The group moved along one side of the chapel, still deep in discussion. Then they began pacing out distances and carefully examining a section of the wall, pulling ivy away and tapping the plaster with their walking sticks. After some time, they uncovered a large marble tablet with carved letters standing out in relief.

With the help of the woodman, who had just returned, they revealed a long-hidden monument—one that bore the name of Mircalla, Countess Karnstein.

The old General, though not known for being a particularly religious man, raised his hands and eyes toward the sky, silently giving thanks.

"Tomorrow," I heard him say, "the commissioner will arrive, and the inquiry will be conducted according to the law."

Then, turning to the Baron, he grasped both of his hands firmly and said, "How can I ever thank you? How can any of us? You have saved this land from a terrible curse that has haunted it for more than a century. At last, the monster has been found!"

My father led the Baron aside, and the General followed. I could tell they were discussing my case because they kept glancing at me as they spoke.

A moment later, my father came over, kissed me several times, and said, "It's time to go home. But first, we must stop at the priest's house nearby and ask him to return with us to the schloss."

We succeeded in our task, and I was relieved when we finally reached home, completely exhausted. But my relief quickly turned to unease when I realized there was no news of Carmilla. No one explained what had happened in the ruined chapel, and it was clear my father was deliberately keeping something from me.

Carmilla's strange disappearance only made the memory of that day more unsettling.

The arrangements for the night were unusual. Two servants and Madame were to stay awake in my bedroom, keeping watch, while my father and the priest remained in the dressing room next door. That night, the priest also performed solemn rituals, though I had no idea what they meant or why such extreme precautions were necessary.

It wasn't until a few days later that everything became clear to me.

From the moment Carmilla disappeared, my nightmares and strange illness stopped.

You may have heard of the terrifying legends that exist in parts of Upper and Lower Styria, Moravia, Silesia, Serbia, Poland, and even Russia—the legend of the vampire.

Some call it superstition, but official records tell a different story. Testimonies gathered by countless commissions, made up of intelligent and honorable men, have been documented in reports more detailed than those on nearly any other subject. If human evidence, carefully examined and recorded under oath, holds any weight, then the existence of vampires is something that cannot be easily dismissed or doubted.

I have never heard any explanation for what I saw and experienced, except for the ancient belief that the people of this land have long accepted.

The next day, an official investigation took place in the Karnstein Chapel.

The grave of Countess Mircalla was opened, and both the General and my father immediately recognized her as the same beautiful and deceptive guest they had welcomed into their homes. Though she had been buried for one hundred and fifty years, her face still had the color of life. Her eyes were open, and there was no foul smell from the coffin.

Two doctors were present—one representing the authorities and the other brought in for the investigation. They both confirmed the unbelievable truth: there was still a faint breath coming from her lips and her heart was beating, though very weakly. Her body was untouched by decay. Her skin was soft, her limbs moved easily, and her coffin was filled with seven inches of blood, in which her body was submerged.

These were all the known signs of a vampire.

Following the ancient tradition, they removed her body from the coffin and drove a sharp stake through her heart. At that moment, she let out a terrible scream, just like a living person in extreme pain.

Then, they cut off her head, and a flood of blood poured from her neck.

Finally, her body and head were placed on a large pile of wood and burned to ashes. The remains were thrown into the river and washed away, and since then, the land has never been troubled by a vampire again.

My father owns a copy of the official report written by the Imperial Commission, which was signed by all the witnesses who were there that day. My account of this horrifying event comes directly from that verified document.

Chapter XVI
Conclusion

I am writing all of this, but don't think for a moment that I do so calmly. Even now, I can't remember these events without feeling shaken. The only reason I have forced myself to relive this nightmare is because of your repeated requests. It has unsettled me for months, bringing back the terrible fear that haunted me long after I was freed from it. For years, my days and nights were filled with dread, and I could never stand being alone.

Before I finish, I must mention Baron Vordenburg, the peculiar man who helped us uncover the grave of Countess Mircalla.

He lived in Gratz, surviving on the little money left from his once-grand family estate in Upper Styria. His entire life was dedicated to the deep and painstaking study of vampire folklore. He had read every book on the subject and knew them all by heart. Some of these books had titles like Magia Posthuma, Phlegon de Mirabilibus, and Philosophicae et Christianae Cogitationes de Vampiris by John Christofer Herenberg, among many others. My father borrowed some of them from him.

The Baron had also collected a massive record of court cases related to vampires. From these, he had put together a list of rules that seemed to explain the behavior of these creatures. Some of these rules always applied, while others varied depending on the situation.

One popular idea about vampires, he explained, was completely false—the belief that they were always pale and ghostly. That was just a dramatic invention. In reality, when they roamed among humans, they looked completely normal—as healthy as any living person. Even in their coffins, they still had warm-looking skin, and they showed all the signs of an unnatural existence, just like the Countess Mircalla's body when we found her.

One of the great mysteries surrounding vampires is how they leave their graves and return without disturbing the earth or leaving any sign that their coffins have been opened. No one has ever been able to explain this. Vampires maintain their undead life by sleeping in their graves every day and feeding on the blood of the living.

Another eerie fact about them is that they tend to become obsessed with a specific person, much like someone in love. When they pick their victim, they will do whatever it takes to get close to them, even if there are many obstacles in their way. They are incredibly patient and cunning, waiting for the right moment to drain the life from their chosen target. However, they don't always strike immediately. Instead, they prolong their victims' suffering, enjoying the slow process like a cruel game. It's almost as if they want their prey to willingly submit to them.

But in other cases, vampires don't waste time. They attack without hesitation, overpowering their victim violently and draining them in one swift attack.

The Baron also noted that vampires sometimes have strange rules they must follow. For example, in Mircalla's case, she seemed bound to a name that was an exact rearrangement of her own. That's why she used names like Carmilla and Millarca—each one contained the same letters as "Mircalla."

After Carmilla was destroyed, Baron Vordenburg stayed with us for a few weeks. During that time, my father asked him how he had managed to find the lost tomb of Countess Mircalla, which had been hidden for so long.

The Baron gave a mysterious smile, looking down at his old spectacles as if thinking deeply. Then he answered, "I have many journals and papers written by a remarkable man, and one of them contains the story you speak of—the vampire hunt at Karnstein."

He explained that, while legends often exaggerate things, there was truth to the tale. The so-called Moravian nobleman who had hunted the vampire was not actually from Moravia, though he had moved there later in life. In reality, he was originally from Upper Styria. And there was something even more surprising—he had once been deeply in love with Mircalla herself.

When she died at a young age, his grief was unbearable. But, as Baron Vordenburg explained, vampires do not die like normal people. They continue to exist and multiply, following a dark and unnatural law.

Imagine a place completely free of vampires. How does the curse begin? How does it spread? I'll explain. Sometimes, when a person ends their own life, they return as a vampire. Under certain conditions, a suicide can turn into one of these creatures. This ghostly being visits the living while they sleep, and its victims soon die—only to rise from their graves as new vampires.

That's exactly what happened to Mircalla. She had been haunted by one of these demons, and in time, she became one herself.

My ancestor, Vordenburg, who had the same title I hold now, figured this out. Through his research, he uncovered even more information. One of his greatest fears was that sooner or later, people would suspect that Mircalla's grave held a vampire. In life, she had been everything to him, and he couldn't bear the thought of her remains being desecrated.

He discovered something unusual—when a vampire is truly destroyed, its soul is cast into an even more horrible existence. Desperate to save Mircalla from this fate, he came up with a plan. He pretended to move her body, but instead, he erased all traces of her tomb, so no one could ever find her.

As the years passed and he grew old, his feelings changed. Looking back, he regretted what he had done, and a deep fear took hold of him. Before his death, he wrote down everything—the locations, the secrets, and a confession of his deception. If he had planned to undo his mistake, death stopped him before he could act.

And so, it was left to one of his distant descendants—Baron Vordenburg—to finally track down the vampire's hiding place. But for many, it was already too late.

We spoke a little longer, and one of the things he told me was this:

"A vampire has incredible strength in its hands."

Even though Mircalla's hand was small and delicate, when she grabbed the General's wrist, it was like iron chains locking around him. And her power didn't end there. A vampire's grip leaves behind a numbness that can take years to fade—if it ever fades at all.

The following spring, my father took me on a long journey through Italy. We stayed away for over a year. It took a long time for the terror of those events to fade, but even now, Carmilla's image never truly leaves my mind.

Sometimes, I remember her as the playful, beautiful girl I once knew. Other times, I see the terrifying creature writhing in the ruins of the old church. And more than once, I have snapped out of a daydream, startled—sure I had just heard the soft footsteps of Carmilla outside the drawing-room door.

Thank You for Reading

Dear Reader,

We hope this timeless classic has sparked your imagination and enriched your literary journey. Now that you've turned the final page, we want to share a vision for the future of reading—one where every classic you've ever wanted to explore is at your fingertips, in a format that best suits your life.

We'd like to invite you to gain immediate, unlimited digital & audiobook access to hundreds of the most treasured literary classics ever written—along with the option to secure deluxe paperback, hardcover & box set editions at printing cost. Together, we can spark a new global literary renaissance alongside our small, independent publishing house called "The Library of Alexandria."

Thousands of years ago, the Library of Alexandria stood as a beacon of knowledge—until it was lost to history. We aim to reignite that spirit of preservation and discovery right now, in the modern age—only this time, it's accessible to all, in every language and every format.

Picture a world where every timeless classic, novel, poem, or philosophical treatise is not only available to read but also updated for today's readers—modernized, translated into any language or dialect, and ready to enjoy in any format you choose, whether that is in an eBook, audiobook, paperback, or deluxe hardcover & box set version a printing cost.

By joining our movement to rebuild the modern Library of Alexandria, you become part of an unprecedented mission to offer:

- **Unlimited Audiobook & eBook Access to the Greatest Classics of All Time**

  Instantly explore thousands of legendary works, from Plato and Shakespeare to Jane Austen and Leo Tolstoy. All are instantly ready to read or listen to, giving you a complete literary universe at your fingertips.

- **Paperback & Deluxe Editions at Printing Costs:**

  Purchase any title in a paperback, deluxe hardbound, or deluxe boxset edition at printing costs, shipped right to your doorstep. Curate your personal library of Alexandria with editions worthy of display—crafted to last, designed to captivate, and delivered straight to your door.

- **Modern translations for Contemporary Readers in all languages and dialects**

  Discover a vast selection of classics reimagined in clear, current language—no more struggling with outdated phrases or obscure references. Next to the original versions, we aim to offer translations in as many languages and dialects as possible.

  As we continue our translation efforts and add new languages, readers everywhere can connect with these works as if they were written today. By bridging linguistic divides, you're contributing to ensuring that these timeless stories become more meaningful, accessible, and inspiring for people across the globe.

- **Your Personal Library of Alexandria:**

  Over the months and years, you'll curate a unique physical archive of classics—each volume a testament to your taste, curiosity, and love of knowledge. It's not just about owning books—it's about curating a cultural legacy you'll cherish and pass down for generations to come.

- **Join a Global Literary Renaissance:**

  Your support fuels an ongoing mission: allowing us to reinvest in offering deluxe print editions (including special boxsets) at their true cost, broaden the range of available formats and translations, and extend the reach of these works to new audiences worldwide. By joining today, you're not just preserving a legacy of masterpieces; you set in motion a powerful wave of literary accessibility.

  We are more than a publisher—we're a movement, and we can't do it alone. Your support lets us scale our mission, preserving and reimagining history's greatest works for tomorrow's readers.

Become a Torchbearer of knowledge.

Thank you for picking up this book and allowing us into your literary journey. As you turn the pages, know that you're part of something larger: a global effort to keep these stories alive, share their wisdom across borders and generations, and spark a true cultural revival for the modern era.

If this resonates with you—please consider taking the next step by visiting:

www.libraryofalexandria.com

With gratitude and a shared love of knowledge,

The Modern Library of Alexandria Team

Visit:

www.libraryofalexandria.com

Or scan the code below:

www.ingramcontent.com/pod-product-compliance
Lightning Source LLC
Chambersburg PA
CBHW011524240626
47154CB00009B/2964